MW00935318

Straight A's

Khristina Chess

This book is a work of fiction. All characters, events, and places are the product of the author's imagination, and any resemblance to real events, locales, or persons, living or dead, is entirely coincidental.

Copyright © 2014 Khristina Chess
All rights reserved.

ISBN: 1499620845
ISBN-13: 978-1499620849

STRAIGHT A'S

1. Anxiety

October 2

Mr. Underhill slapped my calculus test face down on my desk.

"The high score on the exam was 15 out of 40," he said as he continued walking down the aisle to the next student. His corduroys swished in the silence.

I regarded the unturned page. If the high score was only 15, maybe it was mine. I'd attempted every problem and even completed a few. Maybe he'd given partial credit.

I was too scared to look.

At the very least, I needed a better score than Heidi Jones. I looked across the room but couldn't read her expression. She wore her boyfriend's football jersey over a turtleneck and his class ring on a chain around her neck.

Mr. Underhill deposited the last paper and returned to the front of the classroom. "Clearly, we're still missing a few of the basic concepts here."

He wrote one of the derivative formulas in the upper left corner of the front board and began talking and scribbling. I grabbed my notebook and turned to a blank page. I copied derivations as fast as I could, but by the third line I was already lost. There were too many variables and numbers to keep up with. From my perspective, the board might as well be covered with ancient Egyptian hieroglyphics describing the weather on the Nile delta. Still, I kept writing frantically with some vague idea that I would study my notes later and somehow make sense of them. Maybe in the quiet hour of 1:00 a.m. I would suddenly discover the Rosetta stone to calculus.

At the second board, Mr. Underhill stopped explaining, and the room went quiet except for the manic tapping and scratching as he wrote. A little tuft of hair waved from the top of his gray head as he added line after line of simplification, each one more confusing than the last. My hand began to cramp.

After filling the front two boards, he raced over to the side wall of the classroom as if he were a skinny game show contestant matching prices with appliances lined up on a stage. He began to repeat the last line from the previous board, but halfway through his copying efforts he stepped back and placed his hand under his chin.

"No, that's not right…" He trailed off, writing ghost messages into the air as he tried to reconcile the formula. His shirt had come untucked.

While he tried to sort out his error, I glanced at my test, which remained face-down on the corner of my desk. Pass or fail? I took a deep breath, closed my eyes, and flipped over the sheet: 4 / 40, F.

My breath caught in my throat. I'd never had an F on a test in my whole life. Quickly, I turned the sheet over again.

My test was a scarlet letter. I didn't want to look at it again. I couldn't think about that. And I couldn't think about whether or not I beat Heidi's score—unlikely! I needed to breathe. I needed to pay attention.

"I made a mistake back there," he said, returning to the front board.

He erased a few variables in the middle of the first board and made some corrections. I tried scanning my own notes to make the same corrections, but I had no idea what he'd changed or why. Plus, I couldn't read half of his handwriting—or mine. Trying to fix my notes would be as futile as finding and modifying an individual pictograph written on the inside wall of the Great Pyramid.

As soon as the bell rang, I ran for the bathroom. Pain clenched my stomach, and my hands shook. I chewed a couple of antacid tablets. Then I leaned against the wall and looked at the test again.

Fail. F.

Red marks slashed across my solutions to the problems. Wrong, wrong, wrong! The marks welled up like blood. For a moment I closed my eyes. I felt so shocked and depressed about my grade that I didn't know what to do. How could this have happened?

Voices in the hall reminded me of the time. Responsibility kicked in. I put the test away and ran my hands under hot water to warm myself. I felt cold, numb, but I couldn't hide in the bathroom all day. The second bell was about to ring, and I had fourth period Physics. That class was almost as confusing as Calculus. I had to pull myself together—at least until lunch.

My best friend Donna met me outside the cafeteria after fourth period. She'd had her blonde hair highlighted and permed again last weekend, and yesterday after school she'd stopped at the tanning beds. Now in her white sweater top and jeans, she looked positively Floridian.

I shook my calculus test in front of her face and wailed, "What am I going *to do*? I've never scored this low on a test in my whole life!"

Donna looked at the page, and her eyes widened. "*You* failed a test?"

"Yes! The whole class failed. The high score was only 15."

"If everyone failed, why are you so upset?" Donna grabbed a lunch tray and stepped into line.

"Because my 4 is a long way from 15." I folded my test paper and shoved it into my bag. "I failed *much worse* than the person who earned the high score."

"Who was that—number two or number three?"

I shuffled forward. "Three."

Tricia Cline—number three in class rank—trailed behind Heidi Jones and me by only a single B that she received in tenth grade. Heidi and I both had perfect straight A's, but I had a slightly higher GPA because I'd taken an extra class last year while Heidi took a study hall.

Donna drummed her acrylic mango-colored fingernails against the plastic tray. "How did number two do?"

"Heidi scored a 10." I made a face.

"See, even your archenemy failed. All is not lost."

"With the curve, she only scored a D. I scored an F. Fail."

"You're going to bring your grade up the same way you always do: hit the books, study, earn extra credit points… All that good stuff."

I knew Donna meant to encourage me, but her words felt hollow. "What if that doesn't work? I think I'm in *real trouble* this time! I'm just too stupid to figure this stuff out."

Donna sighed and rolled her eyes. "You *always* do this! You become so worried and negative about yourself, but it always works out. Just stop it!"

Her words stung. I opened my mouth to protest, but she continued.

"And stop being so depressed all the time. I know that you've gone through a lot lately, especially after your parents separated this summer, but it's time to snap out of it. This is our senior year. We're supposed to be having the best time of our lives."

"Sorry I'm killing your buzz," I said angrily.

"You're killing your own buzz."

I didn't say anything. I couldn't believe she was being so unsupportive and harsh.

"Kim, you only have one senior year. Don't waste it with all this stress and anxiety that doesn't solve anything."

"But you *know* how important grades are to me," I said. "And you know *why*."

"Exactly! Which is why I think you need to find a cute guy to be your Calculus tutor. He could double as your boyfriend. All of your problems would be solved." Donna smiled and poked me in the shoulder.

I stuck out my lower lip but allowed myself to be drawn into the joke. After all, I didn't want to appear depressed all the time. That was no fun. Even if I felt that way.

"But none of the guys in my class are very good at Calculus," I said. "Well, except one guy who also scored a 14—but he's definitely not cute."

"Beggars can't be choosers."

"I am *not* a beggar. Who do you know in other school districts?" I asked, raising my eyebrows hopefully.

"I can ask around. But I'm not sure I know people who know people who can be math tutors. My people know people who can fix your car."

I giggled for real. "Imagine a cute math tutor who could *also* fix your car!"

"We *really* need to find a boyfriend for you."

"I spotted that cute guy again between third and fourth period, near the library."

"Do you know who he is?" she asked.

"No."

"What grade he's in?"

"No idea."

"Do you know anything at all about him?"

"He seems to have a class somewhere around the library between third and fourth period," I said.

"That's excellent detective work," she said dryly.

We shuffled forward in line and put our trays on the railing. Food was finally within reach. My stomach felt like a pouch of boiling acid below my heart.

"Actually," I said, lowering my voice, "there's a guy in Writer's Club who's not a joke."

Donna's voice hushed to a whisper. "Really? Do tell."

"He has beautiful eyes. They're the most gorgeous blue-green color—they almost look fake—but I'm pretty sure he doesn't wear contacts."

"What's his name?"

"Elliot, but I just think of him as The Poet. You cannot believe how this guy writes."

"Elliot? I don't know—"

"He's a junior. From California. He just moved here over the summer." So far, the few things I'd learned about him since school started only made him more fascinating. He was someone I might actually want to have a conversation with—not just stalk from a safe distance.

Donna clucked her tongue. "The Poet. I like it."

"Next time I see him, I'll point him out to you."

"If you're so interested in this poet, why haven't you made a move?"

I shrugged. "Because I don't think he'd be interested in me."

"You'll never know unless you do something."

"I don't see you doing anything about Jason," I said.

Donna fluttered her eyelashes. "I'm being coy."

"Uh-huh."

"I'm giving him time to make *his* big move."

She'd been flirting with Jason for over a year. "Why do guys suffer from inertia?" I groaned.

"Hey, don't be throwing your big physics words at me. Save it for your homework." She laughed again, and I snickered with her.

We picked out our food, and Donna pushed her tray forward and handed money to the cashier. I slid into the next line, pulled a free lunch ticket from my pocket, and passed it to the woman. Donna pretended not to notice. Even so, my face and stomach burned.

I dashed into my last class and sat down just before the bell rang. Mrs. Piper was crocheting behind her desk. She was the art teacher and ran my afternoon study hall. I'd taken her Advanced Art class every year until this one, when I'd opted to take Physiology to boost my GPA by a few extra hundredths of a percentage point. Science A's were worth more than A's in art.

Voices hummed all around me as students went to their seats. Cinderblock painted a glossy cream color was the standard classroom décor, but at least here we also had in-progress student paintings to look at. I reluctantly opened my Calculus book. I missed geometry with all its right angles and concentric circles. Geometry had made sense. Plus, in geometry, we had our own compasses. There was something totally supreme about a class that had its own "special equipment." Protractors and compasses almost put geometry in the same league as art.

Trigonometry and algebra had been okay, too. I'd always done well in math. I needed to study it, but I eventually figured things out.

Calculus sucked. Nobody in the whole class understood, and I mean *nobody*! Mr. Underhill was so mad about our terrible scores that at the end of today's class he had passed out two extra worksheets of problems. What made him think we'd be able to figure out the homework when we obviously couldn't work through the problems on the test? He might as well hand out *War and Peace* to a group of first graders and say, "Here, kids, learn to read."

I stared at my Calculus book with determination. I refused to let this class ruin my life.

Someone tapped me on the shoulder. I turned around.

"I heard a rumor about you," Lonnie said.

"Oh yeah?" I tried to be cool. Lonnie Peterson was one of the tough-looking kids who sat at the back of the study hall and played cards every day. He was very cute, tall and broad, blonde, with big hands. He seemed like a giant.

"Are you really the top student in our class?" he asked.

I nodded. Why was he talking to me? And where did he hear this rumor?

"So you're super-smart." He made the statement with a half-smile.

"No, I just study a lot."

He gave me a long look, then leaned forward and stared pointedly at the pile of books on my desk. "Yeah, I've noticed that about you."

He'd noticed me?

"Who's number two?" he asked.

"Heidi Jones." Just saying her name made my lip curl.

He smiled. "Well, you definitely have to beat *her.*"

"Oh, I intend to."

"You make it sound personal."

"I have my reasons."

"Good to know." He leaned closer to me and lowered his voice. A thrill shot through me at his proximity.

"I was going to say you have to beat her for us, because she's in one of the cliques—and you're not."

I gulped. "That's one of the nicest compliments anyone's ever given me."

He shook his head and smiled. "And I think that's one of the saddest things I've ever heard." He waved his hand at my books. "Go, study, win."

I turned around, face flaming. What an idiot. I sounded like some kind of desperate pathetic boob. No wonder I didn't have a boyfriend.

Being valedictorian wasn't so much about beating Heidi Jones—although that victory would be sweet. More important than anything, I wanted to go to college. Maybe to be a writer, maybe a civil engineer or graphic designer, maybe an architect, maybe a CSI tech or FBI agent. I wasn't sure about my major yet, but I definitely wanted at least a bachelor's degree—maybe even a master's.

But the cost of tuition at some universities was more money than Mom earned in a whole year. The only way I could attend a good school was by scholarship, by being at the top of my class, perfect GPA, valedictorian. My whole future rode on this. Everything.

My dad had high standards, too, with his whole "Be number one!" thing. I wanted him to be proud of me. I wanted to win.

I wanted to be able to move to a fun city, where I could be somebody and have a good life and be successful. That meant that I needed to wrap my head around this calculus stuff before it completely got away from me. We were already a month into senior year, and I felt totally lost.

My only comfort was that everyone else seemed to be lost in that class, too.

When I walked into Writer's Club after study hall, I glanced around the room first thing, my eyes searching for The Poet and finding him at one of the tables. He was here. And the chair beside him was empty.

I went over to the filing cabinet with the critique folders. Each writer put copies of their work out for critique, and others submitted anonymous—or not—comments on a worksheet. My latest story had four comment sheets, all positive, and a few editorial marks on the pages.

The Poet wrote, "Great job, Kim! I love it! You're an awesome writer!"

Instantly, I memorized every stroke of his handwriting. I fantasized that his words about my writing reflected his feelings about *me*. Like maybe he meant, *Kim, you're awesome, I love you.*

Mr. Brown wrote, "You can't simply write something, call it fiction, and deem it so because you've changed the name of the main character from Kimberly to Lisa. This can't simply be your story. It must be yours and more than yours! And the further it can move away from yours, the more depth and power it will have. Fiction demands that the writer reach beyond the known into the unknown and make discoveries."

Mr. Brown, also my first-period Honor's English teacher, was our Writer's Club advisor. He was the newest person on the school faculty, only here three years, young and full of energy and ideas. He had thinning reddish-brown hair and a full beard and mustache, and he wore glasses with dark frames and thick lenses.

He had formed a creative writing group during my sophomore year. This year, he had a whole new stack of exercises for our meetings. In addition, we were going to publish three issues of *WordCrafters* instead of two. I liked working on the graphic design and page layout of the student literary magazine, as well as contributing stories. Sometimes I also submitted artwork.

I hugged all the comments to my chest. I could already see how to make changes to my latest story. Half of me wanted to go home immediately and start revising, but the best part of Writer's Club was about to begin.

No one had taken the empty chair beside The Poet yet.

Donna was right: if I was so interested in him, I ought to make a move. I pulled out the chair and sat down.

"Thanks for the comments," I said to him.

"Sure."

I twirled my pencil on the table. I kept thinking up other things to say—and then rejecting them.

"We have a lot to do this afternoon," Mr. Brown said. "Has everyone been writing in their journal?"

A few of us nodded. Most looked at the floor, the table, or out the window. I peeked at The Poet. He looked straight ahead with no change in his expression one way or another. His black eyelashes were incredibly long and thick, giving even more emphasis to his unusual eyes. I glanced away again.

"The best way to get over writer's block is to write, people," Mr. Brown said. "It doesn't matter what, and it doesn't have to be good. Just write. Write in a journal. Write on a scrap paper. Write something. There haven't been many submissions for *WordCrafters* yet. Are you blocked?"

He looked around the room. Writers shrugged. The Poet sat with his elbows and forearms resting on the table, unmoving. He wore a black tee-shirt, and I watched how his biceps bunched.

At that moment, he turned his face toward me and raised his eyebrows. I quickly looked forward at Mr. Brown again. My face was probably as red as a tomato.

"Tell you what," Mr. Brown said. "This next exercise should prompt your creative juices. Who knows what satire is?"

"Making fun of something," The Poet said.

"Sarcasm," one person said.

"Ridicule," another said.

"Irony," The Poet added.

I wondered if he was still looking at me, but I refused to find out. There was no way I could talk to him about anything now that he'd caught me staring at him like that. He probably thought I was a total freak. So much for my big move.

"Good, very good," Mr. Brown said. "Who's heard of Weird Al Yankovich?"

A few hands went up.

"Some of you, okay. Who's heard of Michael Jackson?"

Everyone's hands went up.

"You might remember a little song of his called 'Beat It?' Weird Al did a parody of it called 'Eat It.' Let me play it for you."

I tried to concentrate as we listened to part of the original Michael Jackson song, but I couldn't stop obsessing about that look The Poet had given me. Did he raise his eyebrows because he *liked* catching me staring? Maybe. Or maybe he thought I was a dork.

"Now here's Weird Al's version," Mr. Brown said, and he played the satirical one. Everyone laughed.

When that one finished, Mr. Brown said, "He did another one of Jackson's songs, 'Bad,' which became 'Fat.' Listen to this."

I wanted to look at The Poet again. Could I do it without him catching me this time? No, I was too chicken. Sitting beside him had been a mistake. I could hardly concentrate on anything else—and I *loved* Writer's Club.

"Okay, now it's your turn," Mr. Brown said. "We're going to do a satire of one of these songs."

He held up five sheets of paper with the titles and lyrics of popular songs, and we spent several minutes debating over which song to do. We finally settled on "Happy" by Pharrell Williams. After that, he gave us twenty minutes to write a new song that satirized the original.

"Okay, who wants to read theirs first?" Mr. Brown asked.

"I'll go!" The Poet stood up and sang his new song:

> *It might seem crazy what I'm about to say*
> *Canine's here, and I'm ready to play*
> *I'll fetch balls as fast as you throw them away*
> *And I will dig big holes all over the place*

[Chorus]
Cuz I'm a puppy
Bark along if you want cuz barkin's what puppies do
Cuz I'm a puppy
Chew the shoe if you want cuz chewin's what puppies do
Cuz I'm a puppy
Shred the mail if you want cuz shreddin's what puppies do
Cuz I'm a puppy
Leave a poo if you want cuz poopin's what puppies do

Here comes bad news biting this and that, yeah,
Well, teething's what I got, and my gums hurt bad, yeah,
Well, I should probably warn you 'bout that puddle, yeah,
And I ate something I threw back up
(Sorry)

[Chorus]

Hey, come on
[Bridge]
(puppy)
Sit me down
Can't get me to sit down
Energy's too high
Sit me down
Can't get me to sit down
I said (you told me, "sit down")
Sit me down
Can't get me to sit down
Energy's too high
Sit me down
Can't get me to sit down
I said
[Chorus]

His performance throughout the song gave me an excuse to watch him. His musical voice sounded as beautiful as he looked, and his song lyrics cracked all of us up.

"Excellent, Elliot! That was a perfect example of satire. Someone else?"

One by one, we read our songs to each other, laughing. When it was my turn to read, I felt very self-conscious just thinking about The Poet watching me, wondering if he stared at me the way I'd stared at him, and so I tripped all over my words, face flushed. Still, everyone thought my song was funny.

Mr. Brown made everyone feel like their work was special. I knew that was his job as the teacher—to encourage us—but he made it seem real. He was genuine. He said things to us like, "If you change anything in your work because of a bit of criticism, you must change it because you believe in your heart that it's wrong, not just because someone else says it's wrong—even if that someone is a teacher."

Too soon, it was time to go home. I went out to my car. It was the only positive thing to come out of my parents' separation, and I'd gladly give it up if they'd get back together. Dad insisted on buying me a used car so that I could visit him anytime I wanted. It wasn't much to look at, but at least it was reliable and passed state inspection.

In the rearview mirror, I met my own baby-blue eyes, highlighted with black mascara and eyeliner. My strawberry blonde hair hung in straight layers that framed my face and went down to the middle of my back. Freckles dotted my nose. I stuck out my tongue at myself and grinned. I felt totally excited about writing. I hadn't written much all summer, though I did some revising on my old stories. Now I wanted to create something brand new—and I also wanted to revise my story based on the comments from the other writers. But first, I had four quizzes tomorrow to study for and homework due in every subject: Calculus, Honors English, Physics, Physiology, and Economics.

2. Academics

October 14

The next week and a half passed in a blur. I had a major paper due in English and also wrote a new short story for Writer's Club. I earned low A's on my next exams in both Physics and Calculus—proving to myself that I wasn't an idiot, but not bringing up my overall grades.

No need for panic yet. November 4—the end of the grading period—was still three weeks away.

In Writer's Club, The Poet wrote glowing comments on my work, but I never caught him glancing my way. Whenever he sat at the same table with me, he acted unaware of my presence.

He obviously wanted nothing to do with me.

But I couldn't help watching him. Every day, I looked for him in the cafeteria and in the hall between classes. Unexpected glimpses of his face gave me belly-flipping thrills.

On the following Tuesday morning, I stopped by Writer's Club and checked the writer's corner for new submissions before first period. There were two new poems by The Poet. I grabbed them and a blank comment sheet and headed to my first class of the day, which was Honor's English with Mr. Brown.

I read them while the other students took their seats. My favorite was the one titled "Paris Goes to Harvard."

Paris left for Harvard today. She went to find a man.
She wants to find a brain there too—though doubtful that she can.
She's got some smarts, don't get me wrong, and just the kind she needs
To get through life without much strife, not needing much to read.

Her parents are quite loaded, and her bra size double D.
She's blonde and fine to look at—though not hers naturally.
I bet she snags some frat boy on his way to Harvard Law.
Before she's done with him, those boobs will stick inside his craw.

Paris plans to wed a rich man, a special kind of guy.
She wants a pedigree with money and twinkling blue eyes.
She thinks she's got it all figured out. Yes, she knows the game.
She forgets that others know it too. They're playing just the same.

Mr. Brown started talking, but I kept thinking about the poem, and The Poet, and how clever he was. How funny, and gorgeous, and interesting, and creative, and mysterious. I wondered if he was thinking about a specific person when he wrote about Paris—maybe someone he knew from his previous school.

"What is success?" Mr. Brown asked. "Kim, what do you think?"

I jumped, not accustomed to being called on at the beginning of the discussion. Eyes turned to look at me. I felt color rushing to my cheeks and ducked my head. I hated being fair-skinned. Everyone always knew my emotional state.

"Um, success?" I cleared my throat. "A stable career, money, and family. Those three things usually define success."

"Ah yes, money!" Mr. Brown said. He turned and walked toward the other end of the classroom. I casually slid the poem into one of my notebooks. "Everyone equates *money* with success in this culture. If you don't live in a nice house and drive a nice car, does that mean you're not successful?"

Everyone shouted at once. "No! Yes!"

Mr. Brown raised his eyebrows above the dark frames of his glasses and looked at us.

I thought about my parents and how much my mom worried about money. Everything about me cost money. My doctor's visits and prescriptions cost money. Senior pictures cost money. Gas to drive back and forth to school cost money. Car insurance cost money. The freaking laundromat to wash my clothes cost money.

Yes, money was essential to success. I didn't have to be filthy rich as an adult, but I wanted enough money to support myself and not have to depend on anyone else.

"I want to be a millionaire," one guy said.

"I want to drive a Porsche," another said.

"Kim," Mr. Brown said, turning back to me, "you also mentioned that 'a stable career' was part of your formula for success. Can you elaborate on that?"

"I just meant that I don't ever want to have to worry about unemployment," I said. "I want a recession-proof type of job, like engineering or medicine, so that I don't get laid off."

"So unemployed people are not successful?" he asked me.

"No."

"You have to have a job to be successful?"

"Yes."

He headed toward the other side of the room again. "Does everyone else believe this, too?"

Most people nodded.

"Heidi, you don't seem to agree," Mr. Brown said.

Heidi flung her long, curly hair over her shoulder and shook her head. "Saying that you have to have a job to be successful implies that money is the primary measurement of success. But that's not true. People are successful at all kinds of things that don't revolve around money, and, therefore, they don't have to be employed to be a success. A stay-at-home Mom can be a successful Den Mother for her local Girl Scout Chapter or a volunteer soccer coach or any number of things."

Who was *she* to say that money wasn't an important measure of success? Someone whose family had lots of money could afford to take the high road on the issue.

"Excellent point," Mr. Brown said.

"Yeah, but is the soccer Mom as successful as the Wall Street banker?" I asked.

"Good question. How do you measure success?" Mr. Brown stroked his beard thoughtfully.

"Success is individual," she said.

"It's also societal," I said.

"So you're saying the soccer Mom's not valuable?" she asked me.

"No, by definition she's not. Value is the *worth* that a society places on something in terms of money. By definition, the soccer mom doesn't have the same *net worth* as the Wall Street banker because she hasn't attained the same level of wealth."

"Who else wants to weigh in?" Mr. Brown asked. "We have wealth, fame, and job title…what other measures of success are there?"

"Power," one guy said.

"Happiness," someone else said.

"And money buys happiness, right?" Mr. Brown asked.

"Not necessarily."

"The Wall Street banker might be on the verge of suicide because he's been embezzling money," another person pointed out.

"The soccer Mom might be a secret alcoholic," someone added.

"Maybe you can't measure success."

"Maybe it doesn't exist."

The discussion continued for the entire first period. Once Mr. Brown started us, he didn't need to call on anyone else except a few of the shy people. Otherwise, he just threw out provocative questions to keep everyone stirred up.

At the end of the class, Mr. Brown returned our book reports.

"See me after class," he said when he placed mine on my desk. I'd written on Sylvia Plath's *The Bell Jar* and received a high A, despite two stupid grammatical errors. I couldn't imagine what he wanted to talk to me about.

I jiggled my foot, eager to leave because I always spotted The Poet in the hall after this class, and I didn't want to miss him. As the room emptied, I walked to Mr. Brown's desk. "What's up?" I asked.

He pointed at the paper in my hands. "What made you choose Sylvia Plath for your report?" he asked.

I shrugged. "I don't know. I heard it was a good book."

"You did a really good job with it. Your writing is college-level material."

"Thanks."

He tilted his head slightly to the side and asked, "What about Virginia Woolf? Why did you choose her for your last project?"

"She's a classic author."

"Both Woolf and Plath are also famous suicides. So was Hemingway, by the way. I was just wondering if the pattern was intentional."

"No, it wasn't."

We stared at one another in silence. I didn't like to lie to Mr. Brown, but he also couldn't know the truth. It made me seem crazy. I supposed this meant I couldn't choose Anne Sexton, Hart Crane, or David Foster Wallace for my next projects.

"Are you sure everything's okay, Kim? You haven't seemed like yourself lately."

"I'm *fine!*"

I wrote fiction, which made me a pretty good storyteller, both on the page and in real life, but today I felt like he could read my mind and knew that I sometimes spent nights crying and writing sad poems—and that I'd written in my journal about suicide. I didn't want him to know that. No one could know. It was a secret.

"How are things at home?" he asked.

I looked at the ground. He really could read minds.

"Kim?"

I liked Mr. Brown well enough to at least give him an answer. "My parents separated last summer."

"Oh, I'm sorry to hear that." His voice softened with kindness. "How are you doing?"

I shrugged. "I'm trying really hard not to be judgmental or choose sides—though it's hard. I feel like it should be their problem, not mine, you know?" He nodded, so I continued. "Besides, I have plenty of *my own* problems to deal with right now."

"Like what?"

"Like *my grades*."

"Are you having some problems in school this year?" He looked concerned.

"A little," I admitted. "With Calculus and Physics…but I know I'll be able to bring my scores up before the end of the grading period." That's the story I kept telling myself. I thought that if I kept repeating it, it might come true.

He folded his arms across his chest and nodded. "Hmm. That explains some things."

"Like what?" I asked, suspicious.

"It's just that your stories have had some pretty disturbing themes lately. The protagonist in 'Barn Dancer' was a pyromaniac who set a barn and himself on fire. 'Under the Trestle' involved throwing a kid off a railroad bridge. And that other one about—"

"'Under the Trestle' is about a murder, not suicide." I tried to change the subject. "By the way, did I tell you about that magazine rejection? They said something like, 'Kimberly, these are great, but I can't see our printing a story with <u>dead parents</u>. Some of our readers are too young. Thanks for writing.'"

"See what I mean? What's with all this morbidity?"

He seemed to be way too close to seeing the truth. I felt panic inside but shrugged. "Don't you always tell us to write what we know?"

"And all you know is darkness?"

Not exactly. My heart chased one spot of light—so small it was like a firefly.

"Do you really want me to write sappy teen love poems?" I asked.

"At this point, that would be refreshing, yes."

"I'll make you sorry you said that." I grinned.

Mr. Brown smiled, too. "Bring it on."

I looked at my watch. "I'm going to be late for Gym."

"Seriously, Kim, if you ever need to talk—"

"I know. I'm fine."

"Okay, well, good paper. Try someone a little more upbeat for your next author. Maybe Steinbeck and good old *Grapes of Wrath*."

"Ha. Ha."

"See, you're smiling. I'm feeling better about you already. Get out of here."

I hurried out of the room, but I didn't catch my usual glimpse of The Poet on my way to Gym. Where was he? He always stood outside his classroom until the bell rang. I guessed I was just too late; I barely had enough time to change for class, but with all the rushing around, at least I was warmed up and ready to play.

I thought about him the whole Gym period, wondering why he wasn't there.

The rest of my day went downhill after that. Third period was Calculus with Mr. Underhill. He gave a pop quiz with two questions. We had to reproduce the proofs he'd gone over in class the day before. I only knew how to do one of them the whole way through. Fifty percent was another F.

Heidi, on the other hand, looked confident and happy when she turned in her paper. With my luck, she'd hired a math tutor, and the class curve was about to go up—sealing my fate.

Fourth period was Physics with Mrs. Lynch, who spent the next hour on vectors, scalars, acceleration, and motion. Her board began looking a lot like Mr. Underhill's. Neither class made much sense. I copied down graphs and equations I did not understand. She announced another test in two days.

After the bell, I met Donna and some other friends at the cafeteria. They were talking about a guy who'd totaled his car on Sunday and had been discharged from the hospital yesterday. I didn't know him. They said he'd been completely wasted and was lucky to be alive.

I scanned the lunch room for The Poet, but he wasn't sitting with his friends. Was he out sick? In a car wreck? Was that why I'd missed him before Gym this morning?

I always looked forward to seeing him at Writer's Club meetings. It wouldn't be the same if he didn't show up today.

I sat through the entire lunch period and waited anxiously for him to show up, but he didn't come.

Fifth period was physiology with Mr. Homes in the science hall. Except for the formaldehyde and dead animal smell, this class was great. Memorization of skeletal, nervous, vascular, and muscular systems was easy. I could name every bone in the human body. Maybe I needed to go to college to be a Medical Examiner or Coroner.

After sixth period Economics class, I met Donna at her locker, where we exchanged notes and a few laughs before I headed into my seventh period study hall.

Mrs. Piper sat behind her desk with a cup of hot tea and her crocheting. Acrylic paintings from the fifth period class leaned against the heater behind her, drying. They depicted colorful clown faces but were incomplete. I wanted to paint one, too.

Before starting homework, I re-read "Paris Goes to Harvard" and wrote up my critique comments to leave at the writer's corner for The Poet—just in case he came to school late and showed up for Writer's Club after all. Then I opened my physics book and looked at my notes from Mrs. Lynch's class. It *looked like* trigonometry. It should have made more sense. It was just a graph.

My mood shifted in an instant. Tears burned my eyes, and I blinked fast. I couldn't cry in study hall! Why was I so confused? Why couldn't my brain make sense of anything? Why was I so stupid?

The hope I'd had at the beginning of the day vanished. I had plenty of reason to panic. November 4 was *only three weeks away*! I'd just bombed another Calculus quiz, when I needed to earn perfect scores to bring my B's up to A's.

Stupid! Stupid! Stupid!

Our Physics class was so rowdy that the teacher didn't always have time to go over all of the assigned homework problems, and then I had to spend hours at night trying to figure out how to do them by myself. And I couldn't. I just couldn't. And I *hated it* when I didn't understand! Lately my brain turned into oatmeal when I most needed to focus. I had trouble concentrating—even with the easier classes like economics and physiology, even after taking caffeine pills and drinking a gallon of iced tea. What was *wrong* with me? I never used to be this way. How was I going to catch up before report cards came out?

I looked across the room at William, the nerdy guy who'd scored the 14 on that first calculus test and who was number four in our class rank. Donna and I had joked about finding a tutor for me. But what if I asked for help? What if I still couldn't understand it, even when he was explaining it to me? What if he thought I was a stupid idiot? Then I'd be an even bigger failure than I already was.

I stared at him and thought about it until the bell. Then I closed my notebook and went to Writer's Club. I dropped my comments into The Poet's folder and looked around, but he didn't come. I should have known when I didn't see him at lunch, but I'd kept hoping for that, too. Everything was wrong today.

When I got home from school that afternoon, I could tell by the expression on Mom's face that she'd had another Bad Day at work. She wore an old sweatshirt and sat in front of the TV, smoking. She looked tired, in her own world, sad. I didn't smell anything cooking for dinner. I guessed it was everyone-for-themselves night again.

"Anyone call for me?" I kicked off my shoes at the door.

"Your father."

I took off my coat slowly. "What did he want?"

She exhaled a long stream of smoke. "I didn't chitchat with him."

"He really misses you, you know," I said.

She glanced over at me and said nothing. She didn't care.

"He told me to ask if you'd meet him for coffee sometime," I said.

"Kim…"

I put on my pretend smile. "Now I can tell him that I've asked, and I won't be lying to him."

I went into the kitchen and grabbed a box of macaroni and cheese. I put a pot of water on the stove to boil, dropped my books onto the table, sat, and opened physics to the chapter I still needed to study. Mom came into the kitchen and sat across from me.

She turned my book around so she could read the pages. "Looks like Greek to me."

"Worse. It's physics."

"You've always been so good at science."

"Physics is hard. I keep making stupid math errors on the tests."

"It doesn't sound like you're having trouble with physics then, but math."

"Some of the physics is hard, too."

"I'm sure you'll get the hang of things."

"I don't know, Mom. I've been scoring a lot of B's on tests, and…" My throat suddenly began to burn, and I ducked my head. Mrs. Lynch had returned our physics tests today—another low B for me. "I don't know if I can pull my grade up before the end of the grading period."

I didn't know why I was telling her this. Maybe it was because Mr. Brown had been so nice to me today. It made me soft or something.

She looked at me very seriously. "I know how hard you've worked, all through high school."

"Not hard enough—obviously."

"You know that's not true."

"I can't score a B."

"Kimberly." She put her hand on top of mine, which was flipping through pages at shredding speeds. "It's not going to kill me if you're not valedictorian."

It was weird for her to be in here, talking like this. I wondered what she saw when she looked at me like that.

"I realize what a great honor it would be," she continued, "and how much this means to you right now, but in five years, no one will remember your class ranking in high school."

"I know," I whispered.

"Do you?"

I wanted to throw myself in her lap and bawl, but we weren't that way with each other. She needed me to take care of myself because she had her own problems to deal with. In fact, this night was the first in a long time that she wasn't in her room crying. I nodded at her.

"Just do your best," she said, pulling her hand from mine. "That's all I ever ask from you. I know you will."

I nodded again. I didn't trust my throat to form words.

She just sat there, staring at me. After a long moment, she said, "I worry about you, Kim. You've been spending too much time alone this fall."

"I'm *studying*, Mom. Most parents wouldn't complain about that."

"I know how hard all of this has been on you. I'm sorry."

I chewed on my pencil and said nothing. If she wanted me to say it was okay that she'd left Dad and wrecked my senior year, she would be waiting a long time. I was still mad.

She stood.

"Your water's boiling." She dumped the macaroni into the water for me and set the timer before going back into the living room.

I picked up the phone and dialed Dad's number, but there was no answer. I wondered what he'd wanted and if he was okay.

When the pasta finished cooking, I mixed the cheese and gobbled the whole thing. My stomach really hurt tonight, but food helped, especially creamy, cheesy food that soothed the burning for a little while. I flipped through my physics book while I ate and re-read the entire chapter. I tried calling Dad twice more. I finally reached him.

"Mom said you called," I said.

"Just wanted to say hi. It's been awhile since I've seen you."

"Sorry. Are you going to be home tomorrow afternoon?" I scribbled a black square in the upper right corner of my notebook.

"I'm here every day," he said.

"I'll stop and see you after school."

"Don't put yourself out if you're too busy for your old dad."

"Dad—do you want me to come, or not?" The square kept growing bigger and bigger.

"Yes, I do."

"Then I'll see you tomorrow."

I worried about him. I thought about him sitting at home alone, feeling mad and depressed, feeling like me. Full of scribbled black squares.

Around nine-thirty, Mom turned off the TV and came into the kitchen again. "I'm turning in. How much longer are you going to be?" she asked.

"Another hour maybe. I still have reading for Economics to do."

"Don't stay up too late. You need your rest."

"I will. Mom?"

"Yeah?"

"Are you okay?"

"I'm fine."

We looked at each other. Fine, okay. I nodded. Me too. After her door closed, I stood, stretched, and fixed another glass of iced tea. I couldn't think straight anymore. My thoughts were murky, and I needed to be sharp and accomplish things tonight. I had to write an essay about "What Is Success?" for Honor's English based on today's discussion.

I opened my notebook to a blank page and doodled a flower in the right corner. For me, the path to success started in eighth grade, when teachers put me into algebra and set me onto the advanced academic track. Mr. Jenkins talked to us about college and how important our math foundation was to our future. A few days later, I also watched some movie about a small-town girl who studied like crazy in school, graduated at the top of her class, overcame a bunch of obstacles, and went on to achieve her dream to be a veterinarian for horses.

"That's the American Dream," Dad said to me. "If you work hard enough, you can be and do anything."

"I'm going to be the valedictorian of my class," I announced. "I'm going to graduate number one, go to a top university, and be a marketing executive."

He laughed. "What are you going to market?"

"I don't know, but they make a lot of money."

"Okay, let's see you graduate number one, first."

Dad told everyone that I was going to be valedictorian of my class. He egged me on. All of my parents' friends called me The Brain. It became a challenge I couldn't lose. I was earning straight A's already, so I just needed to keep it up for another four years. No problem, right?

No problem until this year. Now everything was a complete disaster.

I put my school notebook aside and took out my journal. I couldn't concentrate on homework tonight until I pushed this other stuff out of my head. Writing it on the page helped. Writing made it real.

I'm going to do it. November 4 is the last day of the grading period, and if I don't make perfect straight A's, it's all over. My plan is simple. I'll have one week before report cards come out, so I'll write my goodbye letters then. The day that we get them, November 11, I think, I'll leave school right after 1st period. At home, I'll put my report card on the table with my goodbye letters, and then I'm going to overdose on Mom's sleeping pills.

That's my plan.

I cried the whole way home from school today, trying to decide what to do. I've done the best I could, but I'm just not good enough. Being the valedictorian is so important to me and my dreams for my future, and now it looks as though it will never be. I'm not giving up quite yet; there's still a little hope that I can bring my grades up during finals.

Getting straight A's is the only thing that will save me.

If I don't, and I see a B in black and white on my report card, I'll snap. Then I'll know that I've let everyone down—no matter what Mom says. You wouldn't believe how often my family and everyone else has praised my grades and called me the future valedictorian! I'm going to be a disappointment to everyone.

3. Adults

October 15

The next day after school, instead of heading home, I turned onto the road of my childhood and headed toward Dad's house. Every few seconds, the windshield wipers skidded across the windshield and chased away the misting drizzle. A long row of round hay bales wrapped in white plastic stretched across a muddy Pennsylvania pasture. I drove past an old tractor abandoned in a field, dirty cars parked in front of trailers with permanent add-on rooms and pitched roofs, and a barn with rusted metal signs nailed to one wall.

Ours was a two-story farmhouse with white siding and a front porch. This was where I'd grown up. Just seeing the tire swing in the side yard brought a lump to my throat because I missed living here and wanted everything to go back to the way it was.

Except nothing would ever be that way again—not with my parents and not with me.

I wondered if there was some way I could talk to Dad about what was happening. Maybe Mom was right; maybe it could still be okay if I weren't valedictorian. Maybe I didn't have to be Number One.

I parked behind Dad's car and went inside. He was standing at the kitchen sink but turned when I came through the door.

"You want to stay for dinner?" he asked. "I bought a couple of steaks to throw on the grill."

"Okay, then I'm staying for dinner."

"And cooking?" He winked.

I rolled my eyes and put my bag on the counter. "Okay."

"So what did the doctor say about your endoscopy results?"

"It's just an irritation in my stomach lining, not a hole."

"When do you have to go back?"

"I don't. I just keep drinking antacid and eating cheese when it acts up. Plus, he gave me a prescription."

Dad scowled at me. "You're too young to have an ulcer."

We looked at each other for a moment. Then he sighed.

I hated to see that worried look on his face, so I joked, "You're too young to be bald, too—but stuff happens, right?"

"Watch it." But he smiled and gestured for me to follow him into the living room. He sat on his corner of the couch, and I curled up on the opposite end and held the decorative pillow in my lap.

"What are you reading?" I asked.

"I just finished another Tom Clancy, and I'm starting the new Nelson DeMille."

"I'm reading *Sister Carrie* by Theodore Dreiser for Honor's English, and I'm also reading Stephen King's *The Shining*."

"Didn't you read that one already?"

"Yeah, but I'm reading it again. It's a classic! I love the feeling I always have after reading one of his novels because it always inspires me to write. A thousand ideas run through my head for stories of my own, but then I have absolutely no time to write them all down. I always have too much homework to do."

"Welcome to adult life. Work sucks."

"But why does it have to?"

"That's why they call it *work*."

"What if I decided to be a writer? To me, that's not work."

"Why spend money on a college degree to study writing when it doesn't make any money? You might not even find a job, and then you'll be stuck with all those student loans that you can't pay back and a degree that's worthless. Unless you want to *teach*."

He said *teach* as if he didn't think that sounded like a very viable option either.

I traced my finger on the fabric pattern of the pillow in my lap. "But I *like* writing. I'm good at it. I'm not good at physics and calculus and the things that engineers need to be good at."

"We've talked about this before, Kimberly. You can always write as a hobby. But earn your college degree in something you can make a living with: medicine, law, finance... It doesn't have to be engineering. If you still want to study writing after you've finished that first degree, take a few night courses in creative writing or something."

He wasn't yelling, exactly, but his tone sounded very firm. How could I tell him that I wouldn't be able to get that college degree because I probably wasn't going to be valedictorian after all? And if not, I wasn't going to win any academic scholarships or be able to afford to attend a university.

"Did you read my story?" I asked.

"No, not yet. I haven't had a chance."

"Oh." I twisted the tassels on the decorative pillow. He'd had the story for three weeks, and it was only fifteen pages long.

"How's school, anyway?" he asked.

I shrugged. "We're dissecting a cat in physiology class. My partner named him Figaro."

"*You* are cutting up a cat?" He gave me a skeptical look.

"It's pretty gross. I'm doing most of the logging."

"Still getting straight A's?"

I squeezed the pillow against my chest. "I hope so..."

"You'd better *know* so."

"Calculus is *really hard*, Dad!" I raised my voice, trying to make him hear me. "Our teacher is awful!"

"Students always blame the teacher."

Naturally, he would take the teacher's side over mine. Adults always stuck together. "If the whole class is failing— even the honors students—then maybe it's the teacher!"

"Are you failing?" he asked.

"No!" In fact, I had a low B, with the curve, not an F. Still, I felt like I was failing. According to Dad, a B was pretty much the same as an F.

"You'd better not be," he said. "You'd better have an A."

"Or what, I'm grounded?" I challenged.

He slithered his foot across the couch and touched me with his ugly toenail. He'd crushed his big toe when he was a kid, and the nail was permanently deformed—thick, yellow, and disgusting.

I squealed and leaped off the couch. "Dad!"

Grinning, he said, "While you're up, why don't you start the charcoal? I'm hungry."

Gladly, I went outside and dragged the grill into the driveway. I didn't want to talk about school or my grades anymore.

The sky remained overcast, but the rain had stopped. I heaped charcoal into the center of the grating and doused it with lighter fluid. I thought about my short story with the pyromaniac kid who set fires. He loved the heat. He loved the whoosh of ignition. In the end, he set an entire barn on fire with himself inside. I didn't know if he actually wanted to die—just as I didn't know if *I* really wanted to. What I wanted was the proclamation.

Listen to me! Look at me! I'm on fire!

I lit the match and dropped it onto the coals. Whoosh.

I stared at the fire and let tears run down my cheeks. Why wouldn't Dad listen to me? Why didn't he see that I was almost engulfed by the flames?

I didn't know what to do. I couldn't see a way to escape the corner I was in. I kept working hard, trying to study my way into a miracle, but I was running out of time. And tonight, when I tried to paint myself in a different life, one where being valedictorian didn't matter so much, he refused to allow me to make that choice. So I was still in the corner. Still failing.

I had no idea what to do next.

4. Attraction

October 16

On Thursday morning before first period, I stopped by Writer's Club and dropped off my submissions at the writer's corner. I'd written two ridiculously sappy poems to humor Mr. Brown, and I'd spent a lot of time pushing them over-the-top. My favorite one was *Lawn Cowboy*:

> *Afar, I watch him mount his trusty steed,*
> *A mechanical beast of name John Deere.*
> *Easy on the eyes is this guy indeed,*
> *Shirtless and muscled, no bees doth he fear.*
>
> *I long to draw his attentions to me.*
> *Instead, his mind focuses on one track:*
> *The perfect straight line, across yard, to tree.*
> *Naught else, not even sunscreen on his back.*
>
> *One day those six-pack abs will be beer gut,*
> *And hair will sprout in all manner of place.*
> *Trusty green steed will become rust bucket.*
> *Still my true love will shine upon his face.*

If only he would ask me, I'd say yes,
To join the cowboy journey, heading west.

Surely, no one would mistake that for anything but satire.

While in the Writer's Club room, I also checked The Poet's folder for new submissions, but nothing had changed. He hadn't even picked up the comment sheets from Tuesday. Where was he? Was he still out today?

I wanted to see him. I wanted to look into his unusual blue-green eyes and have him smile at me. His smile was imperfect, with one of the side upper front teeth slightly turned and overlapping its neighbor. Adorable. I could be distracted by that mouth.

In Honor's English class, Mr. Brown was talking. I needed to pay attention before he called on me and embarrassed me again. This morning's discussion and essay topic was capital punishment. Our class had students on both sides of the issue, and Mr. Brown had no trouble stirring debate. The class hour flew.

I didn't see The Poet on my way to Gym.

In third period Calculus, Mr. Underhill gave us another pop quiz. This time, though, a miracle occurred. I knew how to work all three proofs on the test and turned it in with high confidence in my answers.

Heidi, on the other hand, didn't look as happy with her performance. I knew better than to hope I'd scored higher than she did.

Mrs. Lynch returned our Physics tests from Monday, and I'd managed a 94, A. I couldn't believe it! Was my luck turning around? I didn't feel any smarter, but something must have clicked because I couldn't fake grades like that. True, most of my problems in Physics had been careless errors in the first two big exams of the grading period. I struggled with some concepts, but I wasn't totally lost the way I felt most of the time in Calculus.

I met Donna at the cafeteria, and we sat at a table with a group of friends. As usual, I bought a package of peanut butter crackers, something small and cheap so that I wouldn't have to use my embarrassing free lunch tickets, and I ate slowly to make them last.

I swept my eyes across the lunch room, looking for The Poet, because I wanted so much to see him at Writer's Club tonight. I spotted his friends, but he was not with them at their table. Where was he?

I looked at the line of kids at the cashier, and suddenly, I saw him. He was staring hard at me. I dropped my head, blushing, shaken by the intensity of his blue-green eyes. Why had he been looking my way, almost as if he sensed that I was searching for him?

"What do you think, Kim?" Donna asked.

I jumped and swiveled to look at her. "About what?"

"The party Saturday night. Aren't you listening?"

"Oh, sure. I'm in. Are you kidding?"

She picked up a French fry and studied me with narrowed eyes. Her long acrylic fingernails—cherry red today—looked like talons.

"What?" I asked.

She popped the fry into her mouth and said nothing. Around us, more discussion about the party continued, and after several moments of weird looks at me, Donna finally turned her attention to the group again.

I picked up a cracker and snuck a glance at The Poet's table. He had taken a seat with his back to me. His thick black hair contrasted starkly with the white tee-shirt that stretched over his broad shoulders.

Donna elbowed my arm and whispered in my ear, "Ah, I see what you're staring at now."

"Shh."

"You need to do something about that."

"I will."

"When?"

I bumped her shoulder. "Hush. Is Jason going to be at the party Saturday night?"

"You know he is."

"You need to do something about *that*."

"What are you two whispering about?" Bobbi asked.

Donna lifted her chin. "Your hair," she said.

"Really?" Bobbi asked.

"Did you cut it or something?" I asked.

Bobbi touched the sides. "No."

"You should," Donna said with a wink.

I finished my crackers and kept my eyes on my own table for the rest of the lunch hour. I didn't need to stare. It was enough that The Poet was in school today. I would see him at Writer's Club. I had all afternoon to think about what I might say.

We could talk about his poems, or what it was like for him to grow up in California, or anything else I could think to ask about his life. People liked talking about themselves. And I wanted to know everything about him.

I wondered what he'd think about the sappy love poems I'd turned in. Would he get it that they were a joke? If he actually thought they were real, I might have to re-think my feelings for him.

In my last-period study hall, I opened my books and bent over my homework before the bell. I wanted to finish as much as possible so that I could enjoy Writer's Club and maybe have some time for writing tonight after I got home.

"No wonder you're Number One," someone said over my shoulder.

The deep voice startled me, and I jumped before turning to look at the speaker.

Lonnie smiled down at me. His blonde bangs fell over his eyes. "You always have those books open."

"I have to. It's hard."

"Why don't you take a break? Come play cards with us today."

I looked at the group sitting at the back table. People didn't usually invite me to socialize with them. Most thought I was a nerd—because I was.

"No thanks," I said. "I really need to finish this. You know, beat the cliques and all that."

He smiled. It transformed his face from tough guy to boyish charm. "Right. Well, we're all rooting for you. And anytime you want to join the game, just come on, okay?"

"Okay."

I didn't understand why Lonnie would give me the time of day. I ducked my head into my papers, ears burning, because other people noticed that he was talking to me and were wondering the same thing.

It was the strangest day. First I did well on my calculus quiz; then I scored an A on a Physics test; then this.

I didn't need any extra help from a tutor. I had this all under control now. I worked through all my homework during study hall and even had time to write a note to Donna before the bell. I hurried to Writer's Club and arrived at the room before anyone else. In the writer's corner, I found a comment sheet from Mr. Brown on my sappy love poems.

"There are glimpses of power here," he wrote. "I've tried to mark some of the better places. I see some wonderful twists and turns, revealing for us the world of adolescent emotion that turns on the sound of a word."

I couldn't decide whether he was messing with me— the same way I was messing with him—or if he truly didn't get it.

"What's with the sonnets?" a smooth voice behind me asked.

I turned. The Poet stood in the doorway with faded jeans low on his narrow hips, a white tee-shirt loose on his muscular chest, and a shock of wavy black hair that framed those stunning aquamarine eyes. Man, he was so…hot.

"Kim?" He took a step toward me.

I startled. "You didn't get it either."

"Satire, no, I get it." He stepped closer and handed a comment sheet to me. "Very good, funny, but…*why?*"

"It's a joke. Mr. Brown said he didn't like all my darkness."

The Poet stopped in front of me. "I love your darkness. I miss all the murder and mayhem. Bring it back."

"I'm working on a long piece, don't worry." Nervous, I tucked my hair behind my ear.

"Really? What's it about?"

"I don't want to jinx it by talking about it before it's done."

He chuckled. "I love suspense. Now I can't wait to read it."

My insides stared shaking. I wanted to keep this going, but I couldn't think of anything interesting to say.

"Don't get your hopes too high," I quipped. "It's just a story."

He smiled. "Every story you write is great."

I blushed and handed him the comment sheet from Mr. Brown, stammering, "What do you think of this? Did he get the joke, or not?"

I watched him read. Those impossibly long eyelashes lowered, and his lips parted slightly.

After a moment, he said, "Yeah, he gets it. But he's right. There's a lot of good stuff in there. You could have written a *good* sonnet if you'd wanted to—instead of making fun."

"I don't want to write sappy love poems."

"You don't *like* sappy love poems?"

I tried to read the expression on his face. Was he *flirting* with me? I blushed again, unsure what to say. "I don't know. Maybe I've just never read a good one."

He smiled with one corner of his mouth but didn't say anything.

"Don't give me that look," I said. "*You* don't write sappy love poems either."

He handed Mr. Brown's comments back to me. Our fingers touched briefly, and I sucked in my breath.

"Maybe I'll write one for you sometime," he said.

He gave me such a dazzling smile that I could only stare at him, blinking and nodding, struck mute.

Voices echoed in the hall outside the door, and then his friend Brandon walked into the room with some of the other writers. "Hey, Elliot, what's up?"

He shrugged and moved away from me. Mr. Brown went to the board with an armful of folders. I hung back, waiting to see where The Poet would sit, in case I could sit beside him, but he and Brandon kept talking. There were four round tables that held eight people. I finally sat at the table that had the most empty chairs and hoped for the best.

I'd had a conversation with him that lasted more than two words! And he'd threatened to write a sappy love poem, hadn't he? Wouldn't that be something? I would start reading all his work for double meaning and drive myself absolutely bonkers, looking for invitations that didn't exist, because that was the kind of desperate, love-starved teenage girl I was.

"Good afternoon, how is everyone today?" Mr. Brown asked us. He took off his glasses and rubbed the lenses with the hem of his shirt for a moment before putting them back on and looking at us.

The kids who hadn't found seats shuffled toward the tables. The Poet sat across from me at the same table. For a moment, our eyes met, and then I looked away, flustered.

"Take out a clean sheet of paper and your pencils for the first writing exercise," Mr. Brown said. "Does everyone here know how to make a banana split? Everyone? This is important."

"I don't *like* banana splits," Amy said. She was another short story writer in the group, a humorist. She was a tiny girl with light brown hair and the worst acne I'd ever seen, but she acted like she didn't even notice.

"Why don't you like banana splits?" Mr. Brown asked.

"I don't think fruit should be mixed with ice cream."

"Do you not *like it*, or are you against it on principle?" He stroked his beard as if considering the comingling of fruit and ice cream a matter of grave importance.

"I don't like the pineapple." Amy lifted her chin. "Strawberries and bananas are okay, I guess, but I outlaw the whole thing on principle."

"Do you know how to make one though?"

"Yes."

He clapped his hands together, once. "Okay, glad we cleared that up. Everyone else know how to make a banana split?"

We all nodded.

"So, here is your writing exercise. A man walks into a crowded ice cream store and claims that last time he received a totally inadequate banana split from the kid who works there. He leaps over the counter and begins to make his own. While he works, he loudly narrates the correct way to make a banana split."

Mr. Brown beamed at us.

"Your job is to write the scene. I'm most interested in the man's tirade about what makes an effective banana split, rather than his strong-arm tactics to climb over the counter. You have twenty minutes, go."

I glanced across the table at The Poet. He smiled and rolled his eyes. I nodded, like we shared a joke. This exercise would be easy; I had this guy. I already saw him in my mind. Now, I just had to transform him onto the page.

Twenty minutes later, I had something silly and fun to share with the group.

"First off," I read out loud, "you have to use the correct serving container for a banana split. It's called a *boat*, people! We are going on a frozen treat *cruise* with this baby. A banana split never goes in a sundae dish."

I smiled and looked around. "Next, the banana. It's a *whole* banana, sliced in half. Not half of a banana, and definitely not banana slices. A whole banana. This is a pontoon boat and needs enough banana to make it float."

This line drew a few laughs. Blushing, I cleared my throat and continued, "Moving on to the ice cream. A classic banana split uses scoops of vanilla, chocolate, and strawberry ice cream—one of each—*not* three scoops of plain vanilla. This is a colorful and flavorfully diverse dessert, multicultural, not white and homogeneous."

"Finally," I said, "we get to the toppings. You must never skimp here. Add a generous spoonful of pineapple over the vanilla ice cream and strawberries over the strawberry ice cream. I recommend two spoons of chocolate over the chocolate ice cream." I held up two fingers for emphasis. "Sprinkle crushed nuts liberally over the whole thing. Whipped cream—always go with *real* whipping cream. Here, you can be creative. Some like to dollop the cream just on the mountain tops of the ice cream, and others like to fill the entire valley between the bananas and the ice cream. Whatever you decide, don't forget to top it off with the maraschino cherry. That incompetent guy who made my banana split yesterday forgot the maraschino cherry. I was so mad I had to come back here and show everyone how it's done. Now you know."

Everyone clapped, and I sat back down. Others read their scenes. It was a good exercise. At the end of the meeting, The Poet left the room with his friends, and I collected a few more comment sheets on the poems I'd written. No one else got the joke. "I'm not writing any more of these," I told Mr. Brown on my way toward the door. "Just so you know."

"Why not try for humor writing? You're very good at it."

"Nope, back to dark and twisted."

"Whatever you do, keep writing."

"See you tomorrow, Mr. Brown."

I drove home. Mom had gone to her therapist's appointment, so I had an hour of quiet to myself. Despite having such a good day with grades and The Poet, I started feeling bad about myself again. I started feeling...gray. It was hard to explain. I thought I had my depression under control, but then I didn't. I thought it was gone, but then it always came back, every night, darkness. Why? Go *away*!

I lay on the couch and stared at the ceiling, watching the shadows move across the white paint as the trees swayed outside the window. I thought about the story I'd told The Poet I was writing. I hadn't started yet, but I knew what it was going to be. It was the story of a girl named Mandy, who was supposed to be valedictorian of her class, except something went terribly wrong, and she killed herself.

Definitely murder and mayhem.

I knew I had to take my time though, and make it perfect before showing it to anyone. I tried to remember Mr.

Brown's editorial comments on my other story. I needed to make this one go beyond my own problems. I needed to push beyond the boundaries of reality into the unknown, and in that place I could make discoveries that would transform my characters and give readers a lasting experience. I wanted to make them *understand* what it felt like to be so depressed and feel like you had no more options in life, like you were in a dead end, and you just wanted the pain to stop. I wanted to make it realistic.

And if I ended up scoring a B in Calculus and taking my own life at the end of the grading period for real, then this story would be my last great opus. It might be the only story of mine that my dad would ever bother to read. Or my mom. It had to be good.

No pressure or anything.

When Mom came home, she talked about her session with her doctor. She smoked and went on for almost an hour about her depression and changing medications and dealing with issues of codependence, and I wanted to scream.

How could she live with me and not see what I was going through, too? Didn't she realize that I was depressed, too? Didn't she see? All she cared about was herself.

"Did you eat?" she finally asked.

"No."

"Is that why you're holding your stomach? Is your ulcer bothering you?"

"A little." I shrugged.

"Bad?"

"Same as always. No big deal."

She sighed and stared at me. I'd had problems with my stomach since the beginning of junior year—thirteen months now. For awhile Mom thought I was just complaining about heartburn, but it never went away with antacids. A recent endoscopy revealed a small ulcer in the lining of my stomach. No wonder it hurt.

"It's a very big deal," she said. "Are you taking your medicine like you're supposed to?"

"Yes!" I rolled my eyes.

"You know you shouldn't skip meals. It's not good for your stomach. Want to order a cheese pizza?"

There were so many things the doctor told me to avoid: don't drink excessive caffeine; don't skip meals; don't get too stressed out. I didn't know how to live that way.

"Okay," I said.

"Call it in, and we'll go pick it up."

After we ate, we watched some TV together, and then Mom went to bed. I wrote a little on the new story about the doomed valedictorian. I didn't stay up too late though.

I went into the bathroom to brush my teeth. Mom's prescription was right there in the medicine cabinet. A pink bottle of Pepto, a bottle of aspirin, some bandages and ointment, rubbing alcohol, and her sleeping pills. I shook one of them onto my palm. What would it do to me? How would it feel? I needed to know—for research. I put the pill onto the center of my tongue, like a single pea, and cupped my hands under the stream of water. I swallowed, looked up, and faced my pale reflection in the mirror.

Maybe The Poet would like me if I had thick, curly hair instead of this thin, straight mess on my head that couldn't even decide if it was blonde or red—so instead it was this in-between color. And freckles—ugh. Who liked those? I looked like a frog.

I turned off the light and went to bed. Boots found a warm spot against my leg to spend the night. I closed my eyes and waited. I fell right to sleep. That's how I knew that taking the whole bottle would definitely do the trick.

5. Alcohol

October 18

When I heard a car pull into the driveway, I glanced at my watch. It was Saturday afternoon, and Donna was coming over to hang out and spend the night. We were going to that party. I'd wanted to finish my homework before she arrived so I didn't have to stay up all night Sunday, but now she was here.

It was time to put on my "Krazy Kim" mask.

Donna and I had once talked about everything, even the hard stuff like divorcing parents, but I didn't feel like I could be real with her anymore. She made it clear that she didn't like the way I was down all the time. But since I didn't know how to put a stop to being depressed, I had to stop being real.

I certainly couldn't tell her what I planned to do if I didn't earn straight A's in November. I didn't even feel like I could tell her I was in trouble anymore, or worried, because that was depressing too.

"Come in," I hollered when I heard her at the door. I stacked my books on the coffee table.

She entered wearing a jeans jacket, a fresh Friday afternoon tan, and pink lipstick. Slung over her right shoulder, she carried a purse and duffle bag for spending the night.

"Just drop that behind the chair," I said.

The brochures from my top-pick college were lying on the table, and Donna picked one up before flopping down on the couch. "Why do you want to go here so bad, anyway?" she asked.

"Just look at it." Lush green lawns and stately academic buildings adorned the glossy cover.

She flipped through the pages. "There are plenty of beautiful college campuses out there."

"That one has a great writing program."

"Is that what you've decided you want to do—write?"

"Not necessarily, but they have a great Fine Arts program, too, if I want to go into Graphic Design—or their Engineering college is outstanding, or Sciences if I want to go that route. They're just all-around great."

"And they're incredibly expensive." She tossed the brochure back on the coffee table. She planned to go for a finance degree—possibly a CPA.

I picked it up. "They have a prestigious name. It will help me find a good job."

"Penn State has a good name too."

I waved the booklet. "This one says *high quality, private university and excellent education*—which translates into a high paying job, which translates into financial security."

"You're making an awful lot of assumptions based on a few pieces of paper stabled together. Someone in their marketing department deserves a raise."

I didn't want to joke about it. I'd just finished my economics homework, and the charts were fresh in my mind. "It's simple supply and demand economics. Tuition there is expensive because the supply is short. There aren't enough seats for everyone who wants to attend."

"Uh-huh." She didn't look impressed. "Just because something's expensive and exclusive doesn't mean it's good. Aren't there better writing programs out there?"

"Maybe Iowa...Emory...Columbia, I think. But all of those are far away. This one is a halfway reasonable driving distance, so I could come home sometimes if I wanted."

She raised her eyebrows, surprised. "I thought you didn't want to come home?"

"Who knows? I might." I shrugged, thinking about The Poet. I allowed myself to imagine, briefly, a future where we were dating, and I would come home on weekends to see him during his senior year.

Donna threw a pillow at me. "Come on, let's go for a walk."

We went outside. Mom's trailer was a beige one at the back of the rental park. We walked the gravel lane to the front of the property. As soon as we rounded a curve in the road, Donna pulled a pack out of her jeans jacket pocket and lit up. I hated cigarettes, which was weird because both my parents and best friend smoked.

Krazy Kim didn't talk about boring things like colleges and tuition. "So Jason's going to be at the party tonight?" I asked.

"Supposed to be." Donna exhaled a cloud of smoke.

"So what's your big game plan?"

"Be cool, available, charming…"

I tittered. "You've done that all summer. It's time to try a different plan."

"How did *your* big plan go with The Poet?" she asked, indignant.

"As a matter of fact, we talked for quite awhile at Writer's Club." I raised my eyebrows and waited for her to be impressed. She was not.

"How long's 'quite awhile?'" she asked.

"At least five minutes. I think he flirted with me."

"You *think*?" This time, her eyebrows went up.

"I'm not very good at this," I admitted.

"You dated Cameron Jenkins for seven months."

"And that's supposed to make me good at flirting? That was three years ago; I was a freshman. Besides, Cameron was a great guy, nice, sweet, but not…*hot*. No one would ever accuse him of flirting or being slightly…dangerous."

"Dangerous?"

"For me, yes. The Poet is dangerous."

She covered her mouth with her manicured fingertips and giggled. "*Oh my!*"

I rolled my eyes and sighed dramatically. "I miss the good old days when I was just a teenage stalker, following some nameless guy down the hall between third and fourth period, keeping a safe distance."

"Now you're—gasp—*talking* to The Poet. What on earth did he say to you during those perilous five minutes?"

"It's not what he said, necessarily. It's just—I could really...I could like him *a lot.*"

"I see. The L-word. *Lot.*"

We reached the end of the lane and turned around. The sky was blue, without a single cloud. A breeze ran through my hair, and the temperature actually felt pretty decent outside, at least in the sun. It was a perfect day. My depression from the other night seemed small and far away.

"That's the problem," I said. "It makes no sense to fall for someone during senior year, when I know I'm leaving for college."

"Do you have to plan every minute of your life? Couldn't you just *date* without worrying about whether or not it might lead to *a relationship* or—heaven forbid—a *marriage proposal?*"

"It's not going to lead to a marriage proposal."

Donna widened her eyes in mock horror. "It might! He might be popping the big question on Valentine's Day, for all you know. You'd better be prepared. You'd better start going over scenarios right now."

"Stop it!" I said. "I'm not that way."

"You are!"

I sighed. "I just don't like surprises."

Donna laughed. "Then you must not like life very much."

The headlights of Donna's sporty red Honda Civic illuminated the reflective paint on the pavement but barely touched the darkness of the rocky cliffs and wooded hills that rose on either side of the interstate. Her long coral fingernails reflected the dashboard lights.

"Can you believe this is our last year?" I asked. "Then we'll move away and never see each other again."

She shot me a sideways glance. "You're not going to go all doom-and-gloom on me again tonight, are you?"

"Nope, I'm going to be totally Happy and Fun!"

"What's with you, anyway? One minute you're up, the next minute you're down. Are you on drugs or something this year?"

"I would never do drugs! You know me better than that." I rolled my eyes. "It's just too much stress. Don't worry, once I drink a few wine coolers, I'll have everyone laughing. You'll see."

"Good deal."

"Hey, open the sunroof," I said as we pulled alongside another car.

She pushed the button.

I stood on the seat and pushed through the opening as we passed a car. "Woooooo!"

"Get in here, you idiot!" she yelled.

"We're going to a party!" I yelled and waved before falling back inside the car, laughing.

"You're nuts," she said and hit the gas. We zoomed down the road.

Once we exited the interstate, Donna drove along a maze of dirt roads to the house. She knew the kids throwing the party. Dozens of cars were parked in front of the place, and inside, the living room was crowded with people and a haze of blue smoke. It was dark, with only a few yellow lamps on corner tables. I followed behind Donna, suddenly shy.

"Here." She handed me a cold green bottle.

I twisted off the cap. The couch and loveseat overflowed with couples—girlfriends sitting on the laps of boyfriends, lots of necking—so we sat on the carpet with another group of people who were unattached. Donna lit a cigarette. She was very cool and sophisticated. I wished I had her social skills. The sweet, fruity flavor of my wine cooler tasted great. A deck of cards came out, and we started playing penny and nickel poker. She'd "loaned" me some money ahead of time—though when I lost everything at parties like this, she never asked me to pay her back.

Soon, I felt pretty good. Donna and the other card players laughed at my jokes. When I emptied one bottle, some guy brought me another. And another. I had to pee, found the bathroom, and stopped in the kitchen for another wine cooler. She smoked and played poker. I dropped out when the cards started to blur.

On Sunday morning, we woke up in the living room at Mom's trailer. I was on the couch, and Donna was stretched across the loveseat with her feet hanging off the end. She'd managed to take out her contacts before going to bed, but without them, she was blind. She squinted in my direction for a moment before pulling her glasses off the floor to look at me. Her hair was sticking up every which way.

"Head hurt?" she whispered.

"A little." I nodded and winced.

"You are such a mess. You crack me up."

Boots wandered into the living room with her tail sticking up in a question mark. She arched her back against the side of the loveseat, purring loudly. Donna reached down and scratched her head. In the kitchen, Mom's smart phone (a pre-separation extravagance) made soft beeping sounds as she played games.

"Did you have fun last night?" I whispered back.

"Sure, especially when Jason showed up."

"Oh, yeah? Did you talk to him?"

"Hello? He played cards with us." Donna sat up and tried to pat down her hair.

"Oh yeah."

"You don't even remember, do you?" She pressed her lips together and shook her head.

"Not really." I sat up, too. My head throbbed. I didn't know how many of those fruity drinks I had. Too many.

"Lonnie came too, and played cards with us."

"He did?"

"You were quite the flirt."

I covered my face with my hands and groaned. "What did I say?"

"You kept threatening to take all his money in seventh period next week."

I groaned again. "Something weird happened this past week that I forgot to tell you about. Lonnie invited me to play cards with the guys in study hall."

"Are you friends or something?"

"No! The only other time I ever talked to him was when he asked me if I was number one in the class, and I told him yes. He said he'd heard a rumor about me."

"Interesting… I wonder who he was talking to—about you."

I covered my face with my hands. "This is a disaster."

"Why? I think Lonnie's cute, don't you?"

"Who doesn't? He's gorgeous. That's not the point," I said.

"What's the point, then?" Donna tossed a pillow across the room at me. "The Poet?"

I caught the pillow. "Yes, *The Poet*."

She shrugged. "Just let it ride and see what happens."

"I don't need this kind of drama in my life."

"Two cute, interesting guys talking to you? Please!" Donna rolled her eyes. "Quit your whining."

She was right. This was a good problem to have. Maybe. At least, any normal girl would think so. But I wasn't normal. I was supposed to be the valedictorian. I was supposed to be concentrating on more important things.

"You want some coffee?" I asked.

She nodded, and we threw off our covers. Then we headed for the kitchen and descended on Mom.

6. Armed

October 20

It happened during class change, while I was on my way to second period Gym.

I felt excited because I would see The Poet for a few seconds. I wondered what he'd be wearing and if he'd notice me as I passed. Just imagining his handsome face made my thoughts go haywire.

I turned the corner and started down the hall where his classroom was located. Lockers lined the walls. Students walked everywhere, and the sound of their voices was a low roar. Two doors down, I spotted The Poet leaning against the wall, hands in his front pockets, watching the crowd, as always.

I took several steps in his direction. I felt suddenly shy and stared at the floor. I was stupid for thinking this guy would ever be interested in me. Look at him. He belonged in a magazine or something. We were not in the same league. Not even close. The only reason he talked to me at all was because of Writer's Club.

A few feet before I reached his classroom, I heard a strange popping sound. Two pops, then a beat of silence, and then screaming.

I froze. Everyone stopped what they were doing. Suddenly, The Poet came to my side and grabbed my arm. "Come on!" he said, urgently.

I heard another one of those popping sounds. The crowd began running and screaming. The Poet's grip on my arm was firm, and I followed him without thinking. He didn't lead me into one of the classrooms but instead pulled open the door to the janitor's closet. I looked at him, confused.

"Trust me," he said.

I pushed past the mop and bucket. He followed me inside and closed the door behind us. The tiny space became black.

My heart pounded. I listened to the voices of students yelling and running in the halls. The popping sounds didn't seem to be any closer to us yet, but they didn't stop either. Now I knew what they were: guns.

Shuffling sounds. The Poet moved closer to me. "Don't worry," he said in a low voice. "I locked the door. We're safe."

I thought about the students in the hall. "They're not."

"Would you like me to open it and let some others in here with us? Someone could stand inside the bucket."

I swallowed. I didn't know where the shooter was, or how many there were. I was scared. "No," I whispered.

We stood silently in the dark for awhile, frozen. Fifteen or twenty minutes passed, maybe longer, and everything became quiet. I strained to listen. What was happening?

Some light filtered through the crack under the door. The floor inside the closet looked pretty nasty, but I thought we'd be hiding in here for hours, maybe all day.

"I'm sitting down," I whispered. "Before I collapse." My whole body shook. My heart still raced in my chest. I wasn't breathing right. I couldn't bear thinking about what might be happening in my school right now, to my friends and classmates and teachers.

The Poet joined me. Our knees bumped. It was impossible to sit without touching. The warmth felt nice. I couldn't see anything except the outline of his face. Of all the people in the hall this morning, why had he grabbed *me* to save?

He had been watching for me.

He liked me.

I was trapped in a janitor's closet with The Poet, and he liked me, and if it weren't for the person with a gun in our school, I might be more excited.

"How long do you think we need to hide in here?" I whispered.

"Until the police come."

"How will we know?"

"They'll sweep the school. We'll know."

There was so much confidence in his answer. "Have you been through this before?" I asked. "In California?"

"We had drills. Don't you have drills?"

"No."

He made a sound of disgust.

"What?"

71

"Kids will be dead because they didn't know what to do," he hissed.

I pulled my leg away from his. This meant cozying up with the bucket instead. "Kids will be dead because *some idiot with a gun* came into the school and shot them."

"But we won't be. Because I knew what to do."

I wrapped my arms around my belly. He was right; he'd saved my life today. "Thank you," I murmured. "I'm glad you did."

He didn't say anything. In the silence, I heard sirens.

"Hear that?" I whispered.

"Yeah."

"Does that mean it will be over soon?"

"Not necessarily. There could be hostages, anything. It could take hours."

"Oh." My voice sank.

He chuckled.

"What?" I asked.

"I didn't realize that being trapped in a closet with me for a few hours would be so awful."

I blushed, but at least the darkness hid my embarrassment. "I didn't mean—"

"I know, I'm just messing with you."

"I'm not at my best right now. Maniacal school shooters knock me off my game."

"Good to know," he said. That chuckle came again. The delicious sound ran up and down my spine.

We listened to the sirens and noise outside the school. We could hear voices and shouting, but nothing specific. No more gunshots had been fired in awhile.

"How big was your school in California?" I asked.

"There were eight hundred kids in my sophomore class alone."

"Wow, we're lucky if there are that many in the whole school here."

"I definitely stick out here like there's a sign on my forehead: Beware—New Kid."

People stared because he was so good looking, but I wasn't going to tell him that.

"You've fit in pretty well," I said instead. "You seem to have made some friends—especially in Writer's Club."

"A few."

"Do you miss California?"

"No."

"You didn't like California?" I was surprised.

"Who doesn't like California?" he answered.

Exactly my thought. "That doesn't answer the question," I said.

"No, I didn't like California."

"Why not?"

"I don't surf."

"Oh." I closed my eyes and thought about him on a surf board, the sun glinting off his tan shoulders, the waves crashing all around him. "Any tattoos?"

"What?" His voice raised in pitch, maybe a little incredulous.

"Sorry, the darkness and terror gave me a false sense of intimacy. I withdraw the question." I hoped he could recognize the banter in my tone. I was trying to be funny, but not everyone understood my joking.

He chuckled. "One. You?"

"Nope. Hopeless fear of needles."

We fell silent for a few minutes. On the other side of the door, nothing moved. What if the police cleared the school and forgot about us? How would we know when to leave? I loved talking to The Poet like this, but I didn't want to spend the whole night in a smelly janitor's closet.

I looked around the cramped space where we were sitting. My chest suddenly constricted. What was going on out there? What had happened? People might be dead— people that I knew. Donna.

Tears welled up in my eyes. I tried to fight them, but that made things worse. I pressed my hands to my mouth to hold back the sobs.

"Shh, don't." The Poet put his arm around my shoulders and pulled me close to him. "Don't go there right now. Don't. We just need to get through this first."

"But Elliot, what if—"

"Nope." He squeezed my shoulders with his arm. He smelled clean and good, no cologne or weird gels, just himself. I liked his warmth and the weight of his bicep. I leaned into him.

I could swear he lowered his face toward my hair, too—and inhaled!

I closed my eyes. My stomach did belly flops. The tears abruptly stopped.

We sat like that for several seconds, not saying anything. Then he murmured, "Did you know that you're one of only three red-headed girls in the whole high school?"

He noticed this? "I've always been called a strawberry blonde." My voice sounded husky from crying.

"Mmm. You're more red than blonde, I think. And the only one with blue eyes."

I sat silent, stunned, unable to believe that he'd paid that level of attention to me and wondering if that meant that he *liked* red hair.

He broke the silence by clearing his voice and asking, "Have you written any more sappy love poems?"

I followed his lead of trying to lighten the moment. "No, I told you I'm not writing any more of those."

"How's your new story coming along then?"

I shrugged. "I'm about halfway through. I hope to finish by November."

"*November?*" I could hear the smile in his voice.

"November's almost here."

I felt like we were moving into dangerous territory. Part of me wanted to tell him everything about my grades. I wanted to tell *someone*, and here in the dark, with The Poet's arm around my shoulders, I almost felt safe enough to confess.

"I guess you don't like winter."

"How did you know that?" I asked, incredulous.

"Lots of people don't, but it was the way you said *November.*"

"Oh."

"Oh?" he asked.

I wished so much that I could see his face. "For a second I thought you were able to read my mind, but you can't," I said.

"Then what are you thinking?" he chuckled. "What's wrong with November?"

"I can't talk about it."

"Your birthday is in November," he said. "And you fear turning into a crone."

"Nope. It's in January."

"Are you moving?"

"No." He was going to guess quickly. My secret was a no-brainer. "Why did you rescue *me*? The hall was full of kids you could have grabbed."

He removed his arm from my shoulders. "I had to save the author. How else will we get the story in *November*?"

I missed his warmth. "That's a lot of pressure for one little story."

"You're the one building it up with the marketing campaign. Pretty soon, it'll be a nominee for the Pulitzer Prize."

"You're angry?" I couldn't believe it.

"I didn't realize you're one of those girls who has trouble with the truth."

"I'm not!"

"Apparently, you are."

I stared at him. I could see a shadowy silhouette of his profile, nothing more. Was he right? "I have a right to my privacy. That's not being dishonest."

"Fair enough, have your privacy."

I bit my lip. He was manipulating me. I knew that. It wasn't going to work. On the other hand, if he wanted personal information, I could give him something.

"My parents separated last summer," I said. "In August."

"What happened?"

"I don't know. I don't think either of *them* even knows what happened."

"And they put you in the middle." His voice once again sounded sympathetic, kind.

"How did you know?" I asked.

"My parents didn't bother getting a divorce to do that to me."

I sighed. "They never seemed particularly unhappy until Mom left. They didn't seem particularly *happy* either, but not *unhappy*."

"Are they getting divorced?" he asked.

"Probably. No one's said the word, but I can't imagine them reconciling."

"Divorce sucks."

"Yeah. I've tried not to let it affect me, but...it has— academically. Report cards come out in November."

"Ah."

"*That's* the problem with November."

"See, that wasn't so hard."

He didn't know the half of it. But still, what I did tell him felt good.

"Tell me about your family," I said. "Are your parents divorced?"

"Nope, just two doctors, unhappily married."

"I don't know which is worse."

"I have a younger sister, in ninth grade, and an older brother, a freshman at Berkeley. He's super-smart, impossible to follow."

"What do you want to do after high school?" I asked.

"Go to New York. On Broadway."

This surprised me. "You want to act?"

"Act, sing, write plays—all of it."

"And your brother goes to Berkeley...I bet your dreams are real popular at home, huh?" I asked.

"Like tuberculosis."

I shifted positions, and our knees bumped again. "Are you going to college in New York, to a liberal arts or drama school or something?"

"Maybe. I haven't decided that yet."

I heard voices coming down the hallway. Radios, boots on the tile floors. We went silent, listening.

"Wait here," The Poet whispered. He stood up and went to the door. He twisted the knob very slowly and peeked out.

I stayed crouched in the corner, suddenly shaking. What if it wasn't over? What if that wasn't the police, but the shooter?

I watched The Poet's outline and waited. After several moments, he pushed the door wide open and stepped into the hallway. He motioned for me to come out too. A police officer stood beside the lockers. He looked into the closet for additional students and then motioned for us to follow him. We walked to the front of the building and exited.

The light was too bright. I squinted into the glare, blinded. Everyone was standing outside. Students and teachers clustered in groups on the grass or around cars. No one looked especially panicked, considering. Bewildered, I wandered around until I found Donna.

"What's going on?" I asked her. "What happened?"

"Where have you been?"

I shaded my eyes with my hands. "Long story. What happened?"

"Tim Maiers walked into school this morning with a gun because Gina Nelson broke up with him. He shot the trophy case up and put a few bullets into the bulletin boards before going to her classroom, where he killed himself in front of her and everyone else."

"Holy cow!"

"So we've all been standing out here for hours while the cops swept the entire school, one room at a time, until they made a hundred and ten percent sure that there wasn't some second psychopathic killer on the loose, waiting to kill us all after we went back to class."

"Ah."

"So where have you been?"

I looked over my shoulder. In my hurry to find her and hear what happened, I hadn't even said goodbye. Now, he was nowhere in sight.

"Kim?"

"In a janitor's closet with The Poet."

Donna's eyebrows shot up and her eyes bulged.

"It's not like it sounds," I said. "We heard the shots, and he grabbed my arm, and he just...he's from California, and they do drills, so he knew what to do."

"Uh-huh."

"It was a safe place to hide."

"Really."

"We just...talked."

"No big moves?"

I bit my lip.

"Spill it," Donna said.

"He might have put his arm around my shoulders for awhile...to comfort me."

"And?"

"Lots of talking."

"And kissing?"

"No kissing," I said.

"Why not?"

"It was a school shooting, not a make-out session."

She clucked her tongue and shook her head. "Still, this is real progress. Good job."

"Yeah, but where did he go? Do you see him?"

She stood on tiptoes and scanned the area. "Nope. No sign of him. He's probably off kissing and telling right now."

"There was no kissing."

"Yet."

"I don't know. I don't know what any of this means. I guess I'll find out tomorrow at Writer's Club when we talk again. I mean, it's not like he asked me on a date or anything. We just…talked. It could mean nothing, you know."

7. Ambivalence

October 21

When I woke up the next morning, my first thought was of The Poet. We talked!

My second thought was that in two weeks from today, the grading period would end. I only had a short time left to bring up my grades in Calculus and Physics.

My third thought was that it was Writer's Club day.

I went to the kitchen and ate a bowl of instant oatmeal for breakfast. I felt excited about seeing The Poet again and wondered what would happen between us at the meeting. Would we act differently after spending all that time together in the janitor's closet, or would we still be the same awkward people we'd been last week?

I drove to school and went to the writer's corner to pick up any new submissions that needed critiques that afternoon. Several students had turned in new work, including The Poet. I didn't have anything. I had made good progress on my new short story but knew I needed to pick up the pace in case I *didn't* bring up my grades in two weeks.

In Honor's English class, Mr. Brown talked about the tragedy of what had happened yesterday with Tim Maiers. He kept tugging on his beard as he talked. He offered to send anyone to the front office for grief counseling if they thought they needed that, but no one wanted to leave. Tim wasn't known in this crowd except as a now infamous name; his close friends took classes like general math, shop, and voc-tech—not advanced placement courses.

I didn't know him either, but several of my friends did. He'd been at that party Donna and I went to last weekend, where I'd seen him and his girlfriend, Gina, talking in the kitchen with some other people. He had curly brown hair, wild and long, and he kept raking it away from his face with his fingers. I couldn't get that image of him out of my head.

With yesterday's events fresh on all of our minds, I thought the class discussion would be about gun control. Who believed a teenager should have access to guns in the first place, let alone bring them to school? But that wasn't the angle Mr. Brown wanted to pursue.

"Why might a person commit suicide?" he asked us.

The class was silent.

"It's okay to talk about this, gang," he said. "We *need* to talk. We need to make sense of what happened here yesterday. Why did this happen? Why!" He banged his fist against an empty desk. A few of us jumped.

"Because his girlfriend broke up with him," one girl said in a quiet voice.

"Yeah." People nodded. Everyone knew.

Mr. Brown shook his head. "How many of you have been dumped by a boyfriend or girlfriend? Hands in the air." He raised his hand and motioned for us to follow suit.

Most in the class raised their hands.

"Well, what are all of you doing here, still breathing?" He pointed at a boy sitting in the front row. "Why didn't *you* walk into the school and shoot yourself?" He pointed at another kid. "Or you? Or you?"

"There must have been more to it," someone said. "Maybe Tim and Gina had a fatal attraction kind of relationship, or maybe Tim had depression, or maybe—"

"Doesn't everyone have depression sometimes?" Mr. Brown paced from one end of the room to the other this morning, very animated.

"Yes! No!" Everyone started talking at once.

"There's a big difference between feeling sad sometimes and being clinically depressed," Heidi said. She twirled her boyfriend's class ring on the chain around her neck.

"Can other people tell the difference between someone who is sad versus someone who is clinically depressed?" Mr. Brown asked.

"Not necessarily."

"Maybe."

"Can the person who is feeling depressed tell the difference?" he asked. He stopped and cocked his head to the side, looking at us.

"Yes."

"Maybe."

"What makes someone go from feeling depressed to taking his or her own life?" he asked.

"Pain," I said. I fiddled with the spiral ring of my notebook and kept my head lowered. "If someone has suffered with depression for a long time, maybe suicide seems like the only way to make it stop."

"Pain," Mr. Brown repeated in a softer tone. I heard him moving closer to me, but I didn't look up.

I wished I'd kept my mouth shut. He was going to ask me something else.

"The kind of pain," he said, "that drove poet and author, Sylvia Plath, to commit suicide by 'placing her head inside her kitchen oven—as if to destroy the very source of her emotional pain.' Isn't that what you wrote in your book report?"

I shifted in my seat. "Something like that."

The class fell silent for a moment. I stared at the cover of my notebook.

"Anger," Heidi said. "That's another reason people commit suicide."

"Elaborate, please." Mr. Brown walked toward the other side of the room, and I exhaled with relief.

"Suicide can be a public statement," she said. "Tim made a very powerful statement when he killed himself in front of Gina and her whole class."

"What did he say? Screw you?" someone asked.

Heidi turned around in her chair. "I don't know. Maybe he said, 'Look how much you've hurt me,' or 'I'll show you.' I just know that he didn't die quietly in a bathtub. I think he was pissed off, not depressed." She faced the front of the room again and crossed her arms over her chest.

"A suicide bomber makes a public statement, too," someone else said. "And a political one."

"Martyrdom, good," Mr. Brown said. "Anything else?"

"Desperation," someone else said. "Sometimes a person doesn't think he has any other choice."

"Give me an example," Mr. Brown said.

"The guy who finally realizes that he's broke and doesn't want to face his wife with the truth, so he shoots himself in the head instead."

Mr. Brown nodded. "Okay, yes. Anyone else?"

"Terminal illness."

"Let's save physician-assisted suicide for a whole separate discussion," Mr. Brown said. "I have something special planned for that. Next question: How do we *feel* about people who commit suicide?"

We looked at him blankly.

"Sad?" someone finally said, quietly.

"That's all?" he asked.

"Pity."

"Curiosity."

"Disgust."

"We judge him," Tricia Cline said.

I blinked. Tricia never volunteered an answer.

Mr. Brown nodded and smiled. "We do, don't we?"

"What a fool he was," Tricia continued in a monotone voice. "What a waste. He was probably on drugs. He might have even stolen that gun." Then she smiled and looked around the room. "We judge him because we don't know how to deal with the really big questions."

"Suicide is a sin," another person said. "It interferes with God's supreme plan for you and your life."

"But how do you know that suicide isn't part of the plan?" I asked. "What if it was your destiny in the first place?"

"Suicide is murder."

"Do you buy that, class?" Mr. Brown asked.

"Yes!"

"No!"

"What if Tim was the victim, not the murderer?" I asked.

"He pulled the trigger."

We continued the discussion for the entire first period. I didn't like how their comments made me feel. It made me wonder how they'd talk about me if I couldn't bring up my grades—and had to make the same choice that Tim made. Would they call me a fool, too? Say I'd been on drugs? Call me a murderer?

No, I had something that Tim didn't. I wrote stories. Right now, I was writing a story that would explain everything, and I would leave it behind so that everyone would understand. They would feel sorry for me then. They'd read about my pain and cry. No one in my English class cried for Tim. He didn't even leave a note.

At the bell, I grabbed my books and dashed out the door, eager to see The Poet before Gym. However, when I turned the corner and started down the hall, a weird feeling washed over me. Everything slowed down. The light seemed to bend, and in my mind I could hear the popping sounds of the gun again. The door of the janitor's closet was up ahead, on my left—and a few doors beyond that, The Poet.

My chest trembled, and I couldn't catch my breath. What was wrong with me? I stopped in the middle of the hall.

I felt like I was going to faint, seriously. And all at once, I knew I couldn't walk past that closet door. Not today.

I turned around and made the long loop through the school to the back side of the gym and locker rooms. It almost made me late for class, but that shaking, sick feeling in my stomach went away.

I wondered if The Poet saw me turn around, and if so, did he think I was avoiding him?

In third period Calculus, Mr. Underhill did a review because tomorrow we had a big exam, and he wanted at least one person in class to score a hundred percent. Several people were doing pretty well now, including Tricia—Number Three—and the guy who was fourth in our class ranking.

I'd run the numbers. If I scored at least ninety-seven percent on tomorrow's exam, and the same on the final, then I could still get an A for the overall course.

Physics class was just as close. I needed to score a very high A on the last exam, as well as the final, in order to earn an overall A for the class.

There was no room for error, but being the valedictorian was still possible.

After Physics, I met Donna for lunch. I swept my eyes across the cafeteria, looking for The Poet, and spotted him in line with his friends. He laughed at something one of them said and shook his head.

Donna noticed the direction of my gaze. "Did you talk to him yet today?" she asked.

"No."

"What are you going to say when you do?"

"I don't know. Stop staring at him."

"He *is* cute."

"I know. Stop!" I pushed her shoulder.

She picked up a lunch tray and stepped into line. I joined her.

I changed the subject. "How are people doing?"

"Not good," she said. "Shocked. Everyone's wondering how this happened. I've heard a few people even try to blame Gina, but she didn't pull the trigger. Tim did."

"Did you know Tim?"

She shrugged. "Just casually. We'd spoken at parties and stuff. He was in a few of my classes over the years. Bob was very good friends with him though. He didn't even come to school today."

Bob was one of our lunch room buddies.

"Have you talked to him yet?" I asked.

"He's not answering his phone."

"But he's okay?"

"I'm pretty sure, yeah. That's just Bob. When he's ready to talk again, he will." Donna pushed her tray through the line. "It just makes me so mad, you know? What Tim did was so selfish!"

"Selfish?"

"He didn't care who else he hurt."

I looked at her profile. I could tell by the way her jaw clenched that she was furious. I thought about how mad she would be with me. There was nothing I could put in a goodbye letter or short story that would stop her anger.

We reached the cashier. Donna paid for her lunch. I bought some peanut butter crackers. Then we headed for our friends at our usual table.

"Hey guys," Donna said to the group.

Conversation started immediately. It gave me a chance to look across the room at The Poet again. He completely ignored me. What was wrong? Was he mad because I hadn't walked down his hall this morning? Or had he changed his mind about me after getting a good night's sleep?

Through the whole lunch period I kept staring at his profile, trying to turn his face with my eyes, but he never looked my way.

Afternoon classes went fast. I obsessed about The Poet. I wondered if he'd talk to me at Writer's Club. When I arrived at Mrs. Piper's study hall at seventh period, I tried to work on my homework, but at first it was hard to concentrate with all those thoughts about The Poet running around my brain.

I flipped to the back of my notebook, where I'd drawn the matrix of my grades and what I needed to do in order to stay valedictorian. That always brought me back into focus.

Number One.

I needed a strategy for tomorrow's big exam in Calculus. I'd have to pull an all-nighter to study. Work every problem again, at least three times. Make sure that I knew how to do them forwards and backwards.

Maybe I should skip Writer's Club tonight. Just go home and study.

No, I'd given up enough. I wouldn't give up writing to be valedictorian. There had to be a line somewhere, didn't there?

I started working problems and kept doing them for the duration of study hall. I felt good about my understanding. If I practiced a few more hours tonight, and if Mr. Underhill didn't throw some weird questions at us, and if I didn't make any mistakes, I might be able to score that ninety-seven percent I needed.

Might.

At the bell, I headed to Writer's Club. I felt eager to see The Poet, excited about writing something new, and happy about my progress in Calculus. It was a good day.

I stopped at the writer's corner. I didn't have any new stories, but sometimes I still received comments on my older stories. There was an envelope for me. Inside was a single sheet of paper, folded into thirds.

> *I wrote this sappy love poem for you.*
> *Please excuse the rhyme,*
> *Infused with copious words to woo.*
> *Won't you please be mine?*

I looked up. The Poet stood a few feet away, watching me, waiting for a reaction. Only I didn't know what to think! Was this satire—or serious?

"So I corrupted you," I said. "Now you're writing sappy love poems too."

His lips pressed tighter, fighting a smile, and then he gave in. "It's a sickness."

"Copious words?"

"*Infused* with them," he said. His aquamarine eyes bore into mine.

Blushing, I looked at the page again. That last sentence screamed at me from the page. But, couched in the middle of this tongue-in-cheek poem, what did he expect me to do with it? Stick my neck out there and see if he meant it in a serious way? I was not that girl.

"You did it," I said. "You've changed my mind about sappy love poems. Some of them are really good."

"I'm glad you like it." The intensity of his gaze remained the same.

I tucked my hair behind my ear and twisted the ends. "Actually…you've managed to pen quite a teaser in four little lines," I said. "Much better than my sorry attempts. People couldn't tell if mine were satire or not, because I didn't write very well, but with yours—I think the confusion is intentional."

"What are you accusing me of?" He widened his eyes in mock horror.

"Good writing?"

"You can't tell if I've written satire or a serious sappy love poem?"

"Well," I amended, "by definition, a *sappy* love poem can't be taken too seriously, can it?"

I folded the sheet of paper and stuffed it back into the envelope. A few other kids had come to the meeting, and I didn't want to share the poem with them—satire or otherwise.

"So you're not taking me seriously?" he asked.

"*You* I take very seriously. This poem, not so much." I smiled to soften the blow, in case I totally misread the situation somehow. And I couldn't believe that I was flirting with The Poet like this.

"What's wrong? Is it my technique?" He smiled and folded his arms across his chest. Muscles bunched beneath his tee-shirt.

Was he still talking about poetry? Or his technique for hitting on girls—if that's what he was doing. Maybe that was just wishful thinking on my part. Probably. I should assume he was talking about poetry, right?

"I'm not experienced enough to say your technique is *wrong*, per se," I said. "I'm just a fellow writer, and reader, giving you feedback. Would you like me to fill out a critique worksheet?"

He laughed. "Not experienced? You're a senior."

"That hardly makes me an expert."

"Not even when it comes to the art of wooing?" He wiggled his eyebrows and smiled playfully.

"Only with cats."

He laughed. "What copious words do you use to woo cats?"

"I find that 'treat' and 'play' are very effective."

"The next time I find myself in need of wooing cats, I'll remember that."

I rolled my eyes.

"Hmm…on second thought, I wonder if 'treat' and 'play' would work on girls, too," he mused. "What do you think?"

I blushed. "Umm…"

"Okay, folks, grab a chair," Mr. Brown said. "We have a lot to do this afternoon."

The Poet sat at the same table as I did. We kept catching one another's glances throughout the meeting. I kept wondering about his poem and its question. Would he ever ask me to "be his" *for real*, or was that just a joke? It seemed that he liked me, but guys could be such idiots. He could flirt with me the whole year without ever asking me out.

Flirting with him was a lot of fun though.

Maybe it was best this way. I had a lot to focus on for the next two weeks with my grades. Dating only got in the way of my goals. Complicated things. And if I didn't bring up my Calculus and Physics scores to A's…I didn't want to have to write a goodbye letter to a boyfriend, too.

"How many of you have been to a play other than the ones here at school?" Mr. Brown asked us.

A few hands went up.

"What happens the most during a play?" he asked.

He looked around the room. Silence.

"Dialog! Words! People *talking* on the stage. With a play, there aren't a lot of special effects. Some, but not like what audiences see in the movies. With a play, the writer must really hone the dialog to tell the story. Listen to how dialog moves the story in this clip."

He played a recording from a scene in *Death of a Salesman.*

"We're going to write dialog today. Two-person scenes, and then we're going to read them. Okay, here's the scene. The husband has backed the car into the mailbox and doesn't want to admit it. The wife wants to know how the fender became dented. You have ten minutes. Go."

I lowered my head and began scribbling. My pen sang across the page. Time disappeared. I went into the world of the characters squabbling over a stupid dent—and lies.

"Pencils down," Mr. Brown said. "I hope you're done. You done?"

A few people kept writing. Most nodded. I was done. Done enough, anyway.

"Now, we read. Let's hear how your dialog *sounds*. That's what we're trying to learn. Dialog is about *spoken* words. That's one of the things that distinguishes it from description. That—and quotation marks."

"Kim, you look ready. Let's hear what you did. Elliot, you read the husband's part, okay?"

I rolled my eyes and felt my face heat. I scooted my chair closer to The Poet's so he could share my paper.

"You write like a girl," The Poet said in a low voice.

I snickered.

"Do you use the cat-wooing words anywhere in this scene?" he whispered.

"No, hush."

The reading went okay. There wasn't much brilliance in a ten-minute writing exercise. I stumbled over my lines and struggled to read my own handwriting in a few places. Mr. Brown critiqued two or three points and moved on to the next writer.

The Poet used "play" and "treat" a total of five times each in his dialog.

At the end of the meeting, I gathered my things. I thought I might walk to the parking lot with him, but before I turned around, he was gone. I guessed he was in a hurry or something.

I drove home with the plan that I'd grab some dinner, take some caffeine pills, and study the rest of the night. I knew I shouldn't do that, but tomorrow was very important for my grades. I had to score a high A on my Calculus test. I just had to. And I *needed* caffeine in order to be able to stay up late and study. It helped focus my brain. I would take care of my ulcer after I won my scholarship for college. Right now, the ends justified the means.

8. Aptitude

October 22

When the alarm went off, I snoozed extra times because I could hardly get out of bed. I'd stayed up until 2:30 a.m., studying. Working problems over and over again.

I drank two giant glasses of iced tea for breakfast. I packed a granola bar and some chewable antacids, knowing I'd want both of them before taking the test. Then I headed to school. Even though I was tired, I felt up, wired, ready for anything. My hands tapped the steering wheel along with the music on the radio.

In first period Honor's English, the discussion topic was cheating. I couldn't pay attention because my mind kept dwelling on my upcoming Calculus test and how well I had to do. Luckily, Mr. Brown didn't call on me. The class passed more slowly than usual.

On my way to Gym, I worried that I might be freaked out again about passing the janitor's closet, but I didn't care because I wanted to see The Poet.

As I approached the place, I felt that same tightness in my chest, like I couldn't breathe. My heart raced. I pushed forward anyway. Breathing was overrated.

The Poet stood outside his classroom, hands shoved into the front pockets of his jeans, wavy black hair hanging over his forehead. He nodded and smiled when he saw me in the crowd, and I smiled back, a little, although I felt in danger of fainting. My head was light and spinning. I didn't understand why I felt so weird about that closet; being in there with The Poet had been a *good thing* hadn't it? I mean, he put his arm around me and everything.

As he walked toward me, his crooked little smile dropped. "You okay?"

I stopped in front of him. "I just feel…weird. Here, in this hall, since the shooting. I feel all…" I motioned with my hands around my head. "I don't know. Like I'm having an anxiety attack or something."

"Post-traumatic stress," he said.

I rolled my eyes and shook my head. "No, it's just stupid."

"PTSD, I'm telling you."

"Nothing really happened to me, except that I spent a few hours in a closet with you—unless *that's* the traumatic stress you're referring to?" I smiled. "Come to think of it…"

"You should go to the nurse. Tell someone." He stared intently at me.

I shrugged. "I'll be fine."

"Well, I hope you don't have to continue avoiding this hall in the mornings, like you did yesterday, because of your PTSD."

"I don't have PTSD," I snapped. He noticed that I hadn't come this way yesterday?

"Trust me, I know things." He winked. A smile softened his face.

I wanted to stand there and talk to him all day, but I said, "I have to go, or I'm going to be late for Gym."

"Okay, see ya."

Flirting with The Poet was great, but still, by the time I reached the Gym, I felt so nauseated that I went into a stall and dry-heaved into a toilet. Nothing came up. Nothing but iced tea. Maybe a little pink stuff that might be blood again. Stupid ulcer. I wiped my mouth with some toilet paper and flushed. My hands shook. I went to the sink and rinsed my mouth. In the mirror, my skin looked blanched and waxy with a thin layer of sweat. My hair hung limply around my face. I definitely looked sick. Not PTSD, but plain old sick. I told the Gym teacher that I'd thrown up and asked for a pass to see the nurse.

I had to get myself under control. My calculus test was less than an hour away.

In the nurse's room, I lay on the cot with a cool towel on my forehead and tried to calm my wild heartbeat. Breathe in, breathe out. My whole body shook. I reached into my bag for the granola bar. I ate that and some antacid tablets and waited. Breathe in, breathe out.

After twenty minutes or so, I felt better. I stayed in the nurse's room for the whole period, and when the bell rang, I went to Calculus to take my test.

While we waited on Mr. Underhill, I glanced around the classroom. Tricia Cline looked calm and prepared for the test. She always did. Like me, she studied hard and kept to herself. She was a brown-haired girl with glasses, sweet and well-liked.

Heidi Jones propped her head against her hand and swung her boyfriend's class ring back and forth, looking bored. She chewed gum. Her hair and makeup looked flawless. She was the lead of the dance team—the high-kicking girls that accompanied the band to football games. Everything about her life seemed perfect.

I wanted to beat her. Though frankly, I'd rather that Tricia beat both of us than for Heidi to win the valedictorian title. Was that too mean of me to think? It was true.

Mr. Underhill's white tennis shoes squeaked when he walked into the classroom with copies of the test in his hand. Cranberry-colored corduroy pants did not match his gray and yellow checkered button-down shirt—which at least he'd tucked in all the way around today. He was tall and slouched as he loped between the desks, handing out papers with a stern look on his face. That expression told us that we'd better pass this time. No fooling around.

I scanned the problems. The first page looked straightforward. No tricks. I flipped the sheet over. Okay. Maybe this would be okay.

I set to work.

The room fell silent.

When the bell rang, I jumped. How did an hour pass so quickly? I stared at my paper. I'd answered all the questions and had just been double-checking my work. I'd verified everything but the last question. I felt pretty good about the test. Ninety-seven percent? I wouldn't know until the grades came back—but maybe. Definitely a maybe.

On my way home from school that afternoon, I stopped to check on Dad. He wasn't home from work yet. I turned on the TV and curled up on his favorite end of the couch. The latest Clive Cussler novel was on the end table with a bookmark mid-way. A hunting rifle leaned against the adjacent wall. The black metal barrel gleamed.

I pressed my face into his pillow and inhaled the smell of cigarettes, my dad. Where was he? I hated the thought of him sitting here and polishing that gun alone at night, sad because his family had deserted him.

My stomach burned. It had bothered me all day. I went to the kitchen and pulled the liquid antacid out of the corner cabinet for a quick swig. A pile of papers sat on the counter. The short story I wrote that I'd given him to read last month was there among the junk mail. Unread.

Dad's car pulled into the driveway. He came into the house with a gallon of milk. I opened the refrigerator door for him, and he slid the carton onto the shelves. There wasn't a lot of food to compete for space. Some lunchmeat, cheese, mayonnaise. No wonder he looked so skinny these days. That leather belt was the only thing holding his jeans up. He wasn't much taller than I, and standing beside him, I could smell his familiar cologne.

He closed the refrigerator door and hitched up his pants. "So when's your mother going to quit playing this game and come home?" he asked.

"I don't think she's playing games."

"Tell her to meet me for coffee."

"Dad, I already asked, like three times. She said no."

He grabbed the edge of the counter and leaned over the sink. "Is there someone else? Have there been any phone calls? Any late nights?"

"No! Nothing like that!" I looked at the floor. I didn't like to think about either of my parents in that way, let alone talk about it with one of them.

He clenched his jaw. After a few minutes of silence, he said, "Well I'll tell you what, little girl. When the bottom finally falls out from under her, and she comes crawling back to me, that door..." He pointed for emphasis. "*That door* will be locked!"

He was scaring me a little. His ongoing sadness was something I understood. Not this anger. Had he ever talked to Mom like this after I'd gone upstairs to bed? What other things had she protected me from? Was this really why she'd left him? I wrapped my arms around my stomach. "I don't want to talk about this. It makes my stomach hurt."

"I didn't cause your ulcer."

"I didn't say you did."

We stared at each other. I knew Mom and Dad argued about pressuring me too much to get good grades. Mom thought Dad pushed too hard, but I pushed myself more than he did. Stress and ulcers just were part of the cost of success.

He threw up his hands and backed away from the sink. "If you want to blame someone, blame your mother. *She's* the one who left *me!*"

"I don't want to blame anyone," I mumbled.

"Do you know what I'm paying on this mortgage that she left me saddled with?" He started pointing at the floor. "And we're not even talking about the electric bill, fuel oil bill, telephone… I'm barely making ends meet here, and I can't afford to start paying child support."

"Mom already said she doesn't want anything from you," I protested.

"Sure, that's what she says now, but once the bills start coming in, she'll be calling the lawyers. Wait and see."

I shook my head. "She won't. She's not like that!"

We stared at one another for a long moment. "I'm sorry, Kim," he said at last, and his voice broke. His eyes turned red and watery. The anger had given way to sadness again. He pulled out one of the kitchen chairs, sat down, and cradled his head in his hands. "If things don't work out at your mother's place, you're always welcome here."

"I know."

He sat still, face hidden. I didn't know what to say or do.

We didn't talk about her anymore. Instead, we went into the living room to watch the evening news. He didn't ask about my grades or anything else about my life—which was good, in a way—and after awhile, I told him I had to go home and study. He followed me to the back door. As I went down the driveway, I looked in the rearview mirror. He stood in the open garage with his hands in his pockets and a fresh cigarette dangling between his lips. I worried about leaving him alone in that big empty house with his shiny guns and his terrible anger and sadness. But I didn't know what else to do.

On the way home, my thoughts about Mom and Dad's separation drifted to Tim and Gina's breakup, which led to Tim's suicide. I worried about my dad's depression. Would he ever try to kill himself? Were he and Tim alike? I wondered if Tim was depressed, or if his action had been an anger impulse. I wondered why boys were more likely to kill themselves with guns, and girls were more likely to use pills. Dad had lots of guns at the house. If I wanted one, I could take one of his. He probably wouldn't even notice one was missing right away. Would using a gun be better?

How did Tim find the courage to pull the trigger? I didn't know if I could do that. In moments of desperation, people found out they could do all kinds of things they never imagined.

Hopefully, tomorrow I would find out how I did on that Calculus test. It would be great if I scored a hundred percent and could just stop thinking about escape plans and all of this dark stuff. I didn't want to die. I'd never wanted that. I just wanted to stop hurting and go back to being my happy old self again.

9. Adequate

October 23

I dreamed about The Poet. It was a simple dream, sweet. We were just in school, but we were a couple, and everyone knew. We sat at a cafeteria table, holding hands, and he looked at me with those glorious eyes of his. I felt mesmerized by them.

I woke up in a good mood.

Maybe Mr. Underhill would return our tests today. Sometimes he graded them overnight, but other times it took two days.

For breakfast, I boiled some water for instant oatmeal. I wasn't that hungry but didn't want to be sick again. I fed Boots some cat food and then got ready for school.

Outside, it was chilly. A thin layer of frost covered my windshield, and I shivered in my coat while waiting for the car to heat up. The sky looked so blue and beautiful, not a cloud to be seen. Bare tree branches stretched toward the sun. I felt optimistic.

At the writer's corner, I picked up several things that other students wanted to have critiqued, including a new poem by The Poet. There was also a sealed white envelope in my folder, no address. I grabbed everything and hurried to first period Honor's English before the bell.

Inside the white envelope, The Poet had left another poem for me.

> *The judicious path less traveled by me.*
> *I'm wearied of evading what I feel*
> *For you. Maybe I surrender to thee.*
> *Careful, girl, I don't know how to be real.*

What was I supposed to do with that? It was the most noncommittal piece of flirting nothingness I'd ever seen. What did he expect me to do? Make the first move? Stick my neck out so that he didn't have to be the one to face rejection?

The writer in me wanted to dash off a pithy poem in return, something clever that would really catch his attention, but I didn't have time for this. I had finals coming up. My whole life was on the line, and I'd always put grades above everything else—especially boys. They were a monumental time waster, like video games, fun but leaving you empty when the game was over.

I shoved the poem back inside the envelope and turned my attention to what Mr. Brown was saying. We had another major paper coming due next week, followed by a final exam for the grading period. I had a high A in this class, but that didn't mean I didn't have to work.

On my way to Gym, I took the back hall and avoided both the closet and The Poet.

In Calculus, Mr. Underhill returned our graded exams. "No curve on this one," he said, smiling broadly. "We had two perfect scores." He placed the first two tests on Tricia and Heidi's desks, so I assumed they were the magnificent ones.

He continued depositing papers around the room. I stared at the unturned page on the corner of my desk for a few seconds. I needed to score at least ninety-seven percent. On a test with fifty questions, that meant I could only miss one of them.

I'd completed all the problems and checked my work on each one except the last.

I bit my lip. Across the room, Tricia looked relaxed and happy; she definitely had one of the perfect scores. Other faces reflected various expressions of relief and disappointment. Mr. Underhill dropped off the last test and went to the front of the classroom.

I needed to pay attention to the lesson. No more procrastination. I flipped my test and looked at the score.

94% A

I scored 47 points of a total 50. My heart sank.

When the bell rang, I left Calculus feeling very low. The odds against me seemed astronomical at this point. Still possible—if I aced the final with a hundred percent—but highly unlikely.

I had to face the strong possibility that I wouldn't be able to bring up my grades before the end of the grading period. I had to start making preparations.

In Physics, Mrs. Lynch gave a pop quiz. I was so upset about Calculus that I completely blanked out and missed two of the questions. I did terrible, and I couldn't afford to do terrible in Physics. My grade was borderline there, too.

By the time I arrived at the cafeteria, my stomach burned, and my depression crushed me like a weight. "What's wrong?" Donna asked immediately.

"It's over. I'm going to have a B in Calculus. Maybe Physics too."

She handed a tray to me. "In that case, you need to eat something."

"I'm not hungry."

"Macaroni and cheese…"

I took the tray. "Finals are my only hope."

"So there's still *hope*?"

"Sure, if I score a hundred percent on the final."

"No problem, you've done that before." She smiled with encouragement. "No parties for you this weekend, young lady. Hit the books." She bumped me with her shoulder.

"I needed a 97% on the Calculus test this week, but I only scored a 94."

Donna put her tray on the railing and turned to me. "Are you even listening to yourself?"

"What?"

"A few weeks ago, you scored 4 out of 40 and had no idea what was going on in that class. Now you scored a 94 instead of a 97, and you're upset. You should be doing cartwheels."

"The 94 does me no good if I still score a B overall. It will mean losing any chance to be the valedictorian."

"You're smart, Kim! You can ace that final. I know you can."

I reached for the macaroni and cheese. "I hope so."

All through lunch, Donna tried to cheer me up, but nothing really worked. I pretended to be okay, but instead of going to fifth period, I went to the nurse and told her I was sick. She called my mom and gave me permission to drive myself home for the afternoon and rest.

I sobbed the whole way. Sometimes it was hard to keep the car on the road. When I arrived, I threw my books on the kitchen table. I went to the bathroom and grabbed Mom's prescription sleeping pills. I brought them to the kitchen and carefully poured them onto the table so that I could count them. There were seventeen pills—one for every year of my life. Would that be enough? I looked at the label on the bottle. There were two refills. I could refill the prescription on the day before I planned to do it. Then I'd definitely have enough.

10. Admirer

October 24

In the morning, I felt better, like I still might win. Sleeping for a solid eight hours helped. While I showered and got ready for school, I vowed to refocus all my energy on preparing for upcoming final exams. In Economics and Physiology I had high A's and no worries, but for both Physics and Calculus, I needed perfect scores to bring my overall grades up to A's.

I could do it.

I *had* to do it—or I would no longer be valedictorian.

My whole future—my *life*—depended on it.

On my way to Mr. Brown's class, I stopped by Writer's Club and checked the writer's corner. Another white envelope waited in my box. This time, it contained a note:

> *Missed you yesterday. Was it the PTSD?*
> *Hope you talked to someone about it.*
> *Writer's Club wasn't the same without you...*

The Poet's words sent a little thrill through me. *Missed you yesterday...* Really? When I pictured his California-boy face, I couldn't believe he even talked to someone like me. And here he was, leaving notes for me.

I shook my head and refolded the page. Focus, grades, finals!

At the beginning of Honor's English class, Mr. Brown returned our latest papers. I scored a hundred. Thank goodness for that, anyway. At least this was one class that I didn't have to worry about.

Mr. Brown tugged on his reddish-brown beard for a minute and looked at us. Then he smiled. "Why are we who we are? Why weren't we born in some rice paddy in Vietnam?"

"DNA makes us who we are," someone said.

"Chance," someone else added. "Chance that the DNA lined up the way it did."

"Fate that our particular parents met each other," a third person said.

"Fate or chance?" Mr. Brown asked. "Which is it?"

"Both."

And so began our discussion for the morning. The time flew. I sided with the group that believed in a combination of fate and chance, though we had strong religious advocates of pure destiny as well as the other side that only believed in random chance. The argument grew heated.

At the bell, I thought about chickening out and taking the alternative hall again, but instead, I headed toward The Poet and the closet. It was a bad idea, but after that note, I was too curious to find out what he might say to me, if anything.

This morning, the anxious feeling didn't crawl all over me at the sight of the Janitor sign on the metal door. My breath tightened a little, but that was it. I kept walking. As usual, The Poet was leaning against the wall outside his classroom. He pushed away and sauntered toward me.

I refused to be tongue-tied by his eyes. "For your information, I went home sick yesterday," I said.

He stopped just a few inches from me and made a brief purring sound. "I'm sorry to hear that. Are you feeling better?"

"Much."

We looked at each other. Crowds of students heading to classes parted around us.

"So…what did you think about my poem the other day?" His voice remained soft, intimate, as if we'd spoken to one another like this for years.

"I don't know how to respond," I said, truthfully. I glanced at his gorgeous face with those high cheekbones, straight nose, and raven-black hair, and my stomach did somersaults. "What do you expect me to say? *Careful girl, I don't know how to be real.* That sounds like a warning I ought to heed."

"Maybe it's a plea for gentleness."

I stared at the ground, which was less distracting. "Oh, okay."

"So…"

"What?" I looked up again.

"Something's wrong." He frowned at me.

"No, I…" I shook my head. "I just have some things going on right now."

"What kind of things?"

He held my gaze, silent, waiting.

He made me nervous. "I'm not good for you," I blurted out. I hadn't meant to say this, but as soon as it came out of my mouth, I knew it was the right thing. I took a step backwards, wanting to put some space between us. "I'm not good for *anyone*. You should stay away, trust me."

His eyes widened. "Where's the gentleness?"

"That was the gentle truth."

He clenched his jaw for a moment, then asked, "Do your *things* have anything to do with report cards coming out in November?"

A jolt shot through me. "What? How…um, no."

"You're not a very good liar." His face hardened.

"The janitor's closet." I suddenly remembered how much I'd said to him in the darkness.

He narrowed his eyes. "Yet here we are, just a few days after I saved your life, and you're already lying and tossing me aside."

"Well, technically, there wasn't a mad shooter in the school, so you didn't actually save my life," I pointed out.

"You didn't answer the question." He stared at me, waiting.

"Okay, yes. And I have to go before I'm late for class." I stepped around him and began walking away.

"I'm not staying away, Kim," he called out after me. "In fact, you can expect even more copious words. It will be my *treat* to *play* with you."

I kept walking. But I smiled.

It didn't last long. In Physics, Mrs. Lynch returned our quizzes from yesterday, and I scored a low B because of the questions I'd missed. After running through my overall numbers, I confirmed that the situation in Physics was as dire as in Calculus. I needed to ace both finals.

Still, I could do it. It was *possible*—mathematically.

At lunch, Donna met me with a huge smile on her face. "I have news," she said.

"Do tell." We stepped into line together.

"Jason's going to be at the Halloween party next Friday, for sure." She clapped her hands silently. Her long, frosted pink fingernails gleamed in the light.

"Hurrah!"

"And…"

"And?" I raised my eyebrows, curious.

"Today I was asked about your…availability."

"Availability for what?" I asked.

Donna lowered her voice confidentially. "Apparently, Lonnie Peterson asked Janet Gordon if you were single, and she asked me because she didn't know what to tell him."

"What did you say?" I whispered.

"Yes. You are, aren't you?"

"I guess so."

I looked across the cafeteria again. The Poet and his friends had gone through the other line and found a table. He sat with his back to me.

"You *guess so?*" Donna asked, following my gaze.

"There's been some more flirting. I'll catch you up. What else?"

"Lonnie also asked if you were going to be at the Halloween party," Donna said. She raised her eyebrows and smiled expectantly.

"And?"

"I said you planned to be," she said. She looked hopeful. "You're going, right? You heard me just say that Jason is going to be there."

"Okay, I'll go with you." I grabbed a package of peanut butter crackers and stepped up to the register. I gave the cashier some money. My hands shook. Why was Lonnie asking about me?

I waited until Donna came through the line with her tray.

"Which one do you like better?" she asked as we started toward our table of friends.

"The Poet."

"What if Lonnie asks you out first?"

I looked at her with horror. "Do you think that's going to happen?"

She shrugged. "You'd better think about what you're going to say. That's all I'm saying."

"I don't have time for this right now. I have to study for finals."

She laughed. "Please, you're as desperate for love as the rest of us." Abruptly, she lowered her voice. "Don't look. He's watching you."

"Shut up."

"What's this about more flirting that you mentioned?"

While we ate, I caught her up on the notes and the poems and the flirting, but I didn't mention that I'd told him to stay away—or his response. Instead, I tried to explain that I didn't have time for a boyfriend right now because of finals.

"How much trouble can one little poet be?" she asked. "Give him a chance."

"I think he could be a whole lot of trouble."

"Trouble can be fun," Donna pointed out.

"Trouble is trouble."

My afternoon classes were pretty quiet until seventh period study hall.

I walked in with my books and sat down, exhausted. For a moment, I stared at the etchings in the table surface. The art room contained six large square tables instead of the traditional classroom desks, and when students worked with instruments like chisels and X-acto knives on projects, carvings inevitably showed up where they didn't belong.

Lonnie Peterson stopped beside me on his way to the back of the room, leaned down, and whispered, "Come play cards with us."

Blonde hair fell over his eyes, which implored mine. He towered above me.

I smiled and shook my head. "I have to study."

"Aw, come on," he purred. "It's Friday afternoon. You have all weekend to study."

"Maybe I have plans this weekend." I opened my Calculus book and reached for a tablet.

"Do you?" he asked, surprised.

"I haven't decided yet." This was true but also misleading. "Anyway, I thought you wanted me to beat Heidi Jones."

"I do!"

I looked up at him. "That means that I have to study in study hall."

He made a low growling noise in his throat. "Smart girls are no fun."

"Thanks for asking though," I said.

I smiled and ducked my head, blushing, turning again to my books. He walked past me to the table where his friends sat. That was weird. I wasn't used to attention from boys. Apparently depression and desperation made me attractive.

I opened my books and stared at the page. My Calculus final was Monday, November 3. I had two weekends and a full week of class time left to prepare. All I needed was a hundred percent. Perfection.

11. Author

October 25

Around nine o'clock on Saturday morning, I put on some old clothes and went over to my bachelor cousin's trailer. Once a month, I cleaned his place to earn some extra money. I knocked on the door, and when no one answered, I let myself in with the spare key. He'd left an envelope of cash on the table and scribbled, "Thanks, Kim!"

I put in my ear buds, donned a pair of thick rubber gloves, and set to work on his kitchen. Mold floated in some of the bowls at the bottom of the sink. I turned on the hot water, dumped bleach into the basin, and added soap. Soon, sweat ran down my back. I didn't want to work at jobs like this for the rest of my life, but if I didn't go to college and move out of this town, that's what would happen. Mom didn't, and now she had to do all kinds of disgusting things at that nursing home where she worked—way worse than handle a few rancid dishes. And they didn't pay her hardly anything.

I picked up the pace. The job took three and a half hours and filled two large trash bags. How did my cousin eat so much pizza without weighing five hundred pounds, and why didn't he throw out the boxes himself?

I went home, showered away the grime, and fixed a grilled cheese sandwich for lunch. While I ate, I flipped through the college brochures again and tried to imagine myself attending classes in those stately buildings and studying on those green lawns. It looked so beautiful. Application deadlines were coming up. I wondered about my SAT scores and if they were good enough for me to be accepted into a prestigious university.

Donna called and asked if I wanted her to come over, but I reminded her that I needed to study for finals this weekend. I spent the entire afternoon in my room and worked through problems.

When Mom came from home from work, I decided to take a break. She changed out of her scrubs and sat in the living room with her cigarettes, playing games on her phone. I grabbed a soda from the refrigerator and joined her.

"How was your day?" I asked.

"Okay. Long."

"Mmm." I popped the tab and took a drink.

Mom eyed the can in my hands. "What did you do all day—sleep?"

"No, I woke up early to clean Eric's place, and then I studied for finals."

"Oh, good." She exhaled a plume of smoke.

It occurred to me that sleeping all day on Saturday wouldn't be a terrible thing; I didn't sleep enough during the week, but whatever.

"I need to ask for a favor," I said.

She eyed me with suspicion. "What?"

"I want to take the SATs one more time before submitting college applications. I think I can bring my scores up a little."

"Okay...what's the catch?"

"There's another test scheduled next month, but I need some money for the fee."

She took a long drag from her cigarette, exhaled, and said, "Didn't Eric pay you today?"

I blinked. "Yeah, but...that's for gas and lunch money and stuff like that."

"Lunch money? You have free lunch tickets."

"I don't use them very often, Mom. I *hate* them! It's humiliating!"

She clenched her jaw. "Going to the laundromat is humiliating *for me*, but I can't afford my own washer and dryer."

"I didn't mean—"

"Do you think this has been easy for me?"

I looked at my lap and mumbled, "No."

"I'm taking one step forward and three steps backward. The alternator goes out in the car. Doctor bills come in. There's always something. I don't have extra money lying around for you to retake the SATs."

Me, it was always me, being a burden on her. "You don't even know how much it costs," I said.

"It doesn't matter because I don't have it. Right now I'm behind on everything. I'm juggling bills, trying to decide which one I can be late on this month in order to pay the ones that are already late. Your test could cost five dollars, and that would be too much."

I started cracking my knuckles. If she couldn't help me with something little like this, how could she help me with college application fees in the spring? Those would be hundreds of dollars. I needed to start cleaning other trailers, every weekend, and saving money now. And I didn't have time to do that and keep up my studies, too.

"Stop it," she said. "That's not good for you."

I dropped my hands.

"Will re-taking the test really help you?" she asked.

"I don't know," I mumbled. "I might not do any better. It's a standardized test."

"But bringing up your score would help your college chances?"

"Yes. Especially my math score."

"Ask your father. I haven't asked him for a dime since I left, but there's no reason he shouldn't be helping you with stuff like this."

I could only imagine how the conversation with Dad would go. He'd complain about the mortgage she'd saddled him with again, and somehow it would be my fault.

Neither of my parents were any help. I don't know why I was thinking about re-taking the SATs anyway. The test date was after report cards came out, and if I didn't earn straight A's, my stupid SAT scores certainly wouldn't make any difference. I should stop planning for a future that might not exist.

I stood. "I'm going for a walk."

"Don't be gone too long. It'll be dark soon."

"I'm not afraid of the dark," I snapped.

We looked at each other. After a moment, she exhaled and lowered her gaze. "I wish you'd stop being so angry with me. I didn't want any of this either."

"How can you say that? *You* left! *You* ruined everything!" Fury raced through me. My heart pounded inside my chest. My face felt hot.

"I had my reasons." She took a last, long drag from her cigarette before squashing the butt in the ashtray.

"Like what?"

"Kim…" Her eyes swam with tears.

"What? Tell me."

"I left because your father had an affair," she said quietly. "And I found out about it."

I felt like she'd just punched me. I shook my head. "No, I don't think that's possible. You haven't seen him. He's lost without you. He was completely blindsided when you left."

"He was surprised to be caught—and I don't think he believed I'd actually leave him."

"He thinks *you're* seeing someone!"

She laughed. It was a short, bitter sound. "Have you seen me go anywhere except work?"

"Bingo."

"Oh yeah, there are lots of single, available men at Bingo under the age of eighty." She rolled her eyes. "God, he has some nerve."

I wrapped my arms around my stomach. My parents weren't ever getting back together again. All the times Mom had gone back to her room, closed the door, and cried the entire evening made sense now—and I felt awful.

"I'm sorry, Mom. I shouldn't have blamed you."

She shook her head and waved her hand, dismissively. "You didn't know. I probably shouldn't have told you tonight either, but I just couldn't bear that look on your face anymore...like you *hated* me."

"I could never hate you." I looked at her, horrified that she could even think that. "You're my mom!"

"Well, and he's your dad, so don't hate him either. This is between us and has nothing to do with you."

I nodded. Nothing to do with me—except that they'd ruined my whole life by splitting up and messing with my home stability during my senior year, when everything mattered the most.

"*Now* I'm going for a walk," I said.

"If you're not back in half an hour, I'm sending out a search party."

"Okay." I pulled on a heavy coat and shoes and headed outside.

I followed the lane to where it dead-ended at the edge of the field. Four-wheelers left a path in the tall grass, and I went that way, too. At the woods, there was a trail that curved to the right and sloped down the hill toward a creek. The sunset was almost complete. Venus was the brightest evening star on the horizon, visible through the trees for awhile until I reached the valley and sat on the big flat rock beside the water.

Moss grew on one side, but the other was bare stone. I leaned against a tree and closed my eyes, listening to the sounds of water falling over rocks in the stream and wind rustling dried leaves.

Sometimes I brought my journal out here and wrote, but it was too dark tonight. For a few minutes, I allowed myself to think about what Mom had just told me, but that hurt too much. What was I supposed to do now? Stop hating her, she said, but I had never hated her. I just felt so…angry, hopeless, helpless, and sad. Always sad.

On the day I found out they were separating, I'd been too shocked to put the pieces together. Donna had brought me home from an afternoon at the lake, and when we walked into the house, my parents were fighting again in the living room.

"I'll call you later," Donna said as she backed out the door. She wanted no part of my family drama. I didn't blame her.

I stood in the kitchen for a moment and let their yelling wash over me. I didn't even listen to the words, just the shrill sounds of their anger toward one another. It was a terrible sound. Then Mom shouted, "This is the last straw! I'm leaving! Kim and I are leaving!" Hearing my name caught my attention.

At that same moment, Mom stomped around the corner and into the kitchen, and we faced one another. Surprise registered on her face.

"Kim," she said.

"Leave me alone!" I turned and ran for my bedroom. I thought that maybe if I burrowed under the covers and closed my eyes, everything would be okay. But it wasn't.

Things would never be okay again.

Now I needed to focus on something that I could control, like my story, which I had to finish before report cards came out. And not only finish—this had to be my best work ever because it would be my last. Everyone would read it. Even Dad would read it. This story wouldn't be shoved into the junk mail pile like "Barn Dancer" had. This story would capture his attention.

Maybe they would even publish it after my death. That happened sometimes. I would become a famous dead author. Not ideal, but still something.

First, though, the story needed to be written. Tomorrow, Sunday, would be dedicated to writing. I thought about the next scene: my character had just failed another major test. She faced the dark night of the soul. She'd discovered her mother's sleeping pills and made a plan to use them if she couldn't bring up her grades by the end of the term. Her only hope was that her sexy hot math tutor would help her understand what she needed to know so that she could ace the test, and they'd fall in love and live happily ever after.

In novels that could happen. But in real life I just had myself.

12. Anatomy

October 27

On Monday at lunch period, I stood behind Donna in the cafeteria line. Out of habit, I scanned the room, looking for The Poet, but since he hadn't been in the hall this morning between first and second period classes, I assumed he wasn't in school today. I didn't see him in the lunchroom either.

"Can you believe it's been a whole week since the school shooting?" Donna asked.

"No, everything's already back to normal. No one's even talking about it anymore."

"The people who cared about Tim and Gina talk, but not in places where you would hear."

"What's that supposed to mean?" I asked, frowning.

"Do you have any clue what they say in shop class?" She raised her eyebrows.

"They talk shop. It's shop class." I nudged her with my elbow. "Get it?"

"I'm being serious."

"Okay, serious. People are still talking about Tim and Gina, but among their friends and in classes that they took, not in classes among people who didn't even know him."

"Exactly," Donna said.

I wondered if I would be a discussion topic for Mr. Brown's English class. Would my friends talk about me at lunch a week later? Would anyone else?

It made me sad to think how small and unimportant I was. Whether I lived or died didn't matter. Well, actually, my mom would be better off because without me, she wouldn't have so many doctor bills to worry about anymore. No more ulcer medicine. No more SAT test fees or college application costs to worry about.

I watched Donna grab a lunch tray, and we joined the line. I thought about the fight I'd had with Mom about spending my money on peanut butter crackers instead of using free lunch tickets because they embarrassed me. That thought took me toward dangerous ground of thinking about my dad having an affair—which I totally didn't want to deal with right now.

New thoughts: Radius, ulna, tibia, fibula, femur, clavicle, scapula…I had to memorize all the skeletal, muscular, nervous, and other body systems for the physiology final. Actually, I'd studied them already for tests throughout the grading period, so it was really just a review. I named and pictured each bone as I went through the body. Maybe I could learn how to solve murders from the bone evidence alone, like that woman on the TV show.

"Jason talked to me through half of study hall this morning," Donna said.

"About what?"

"Just telling stories about things he and his brothers have done over the years. He has this way of making everything hysterical. Like this one time, they bought this old boat and spent months restoring the motor and everything on it, and then when they took it out for a test, it immediately started sinking."

"It's not funny when you tell it," I said.

"Shut up."

At the cashier, Donna paid for her lunch, and I bought my crackers. Then we headed for our usual table. I opened my package and let the conversations of the others wrap around me. I glanced at The Poet's table, mostly out of habit, but he wasn't there. I shouldn't look for him anymore. I told him to stay away because I wasn't any good for him, and I should follow my own advice.

Somebody bumped my shoulder. I looked, and a person was pulling up a chair next to me at the table, although there wasn't a lot of space. Black hair, bulging biceps holding a tray, and then blue-green eyes staring into mine.

"Hi."

"What are you doing?" I whispered.

"I'm Elliot," he said to Donna, ignoring my question.

"Donna." She smiled broadly.

The Poet introduced himself to all of my friends.

"That's all you're eating?" He looked at my peanut butter crackers.

"Mind your own business," I said.

"That's what she usually eats," Donna said.

I turned to her and hissed, "You're not helping."

She shrugged and twisted her mouth. "Oops!"

I turned back to The Poet. "Why are you here?"

"Just checking on you," he said. "How are your studies going?"

"Fine."

"She didn't leave the house all weekend," Donna said. "Nothing but the books for our little valedictorian."

"Valedictorian?" The Poet said, raising his eyebrows. "I had no idea. No wonder November is so serious."

I shot Donna another scowl. "Let's move to another table," I said to The Poet. "Where we can talk in private."

"It will be my *treat* to dine alone with you," he said to me. "But Donna, you and I have to get together sometime, okay?" He winked at her.

There was no way I'd let the two of them go anywhere alone. I gave my best friend a murderous look before heading for an empty table at the other end of the lunch room. The Poet followed me with a huge grin on his face.

We sat across from each other. I stared at my remaining crackers. Why was he here? What did he want? I thought I'd been pretty clear the other day.

"So you have *some things* going on in November—which might have *something* to do with your grades?" he prodded. His eyes sparkled, and he seemed to be enjoying himself.

I shrugged.

"Let me guess... You're failing Honors English?"

"Calculus...And by failing, I mean that I'm getting a B."

"Uh-huh."

"Physics, too."

He nodded, eyes a little wider.

"Unless I earn perfect scores on my finals."

"As in a hundred percent?" He looked skeptical.

"I can do it. I've done it before."

"In a class you've struggled with?"

"I'm studying *a lot*."

He stared at me. The intensity of those aquamarine eyes was unnerving.

"Copious words of encouragement," I said. "That's what I need to hear from you."

"I guess you're not writing then?"

"I am! Writing is stress relief for me."

"When do you find the time?"

"At night, weekends, I don't know. I don't sleep a lot."

He leaned forward, as if he knew his aquamarine eyes might be hypnotic and wanted to use their full power against me. "Let me read some of your pages."

For a moment, I blinked helplessly. "What?"

"Your story." His voice was as smooth as golden honey. "Let me see some of your pages."

I shook my head. "No, it's not ready."

"It might help to have someone give early feedback on the characters and pacing for the first ten pages or so."

I continued shaking my head. If I gave him the first ten pages, he'd know the whole premise and think it was about me. I couldn't let anyone see it until it was done—and not until the grading period was over and the decision about the ending was final.

"Pretty please?" He fluttered his long eyelashes.

"No."

"I'm your number one fan."

"How do you figure that?"

"I've read all of your stuff, sometimes more than once."

"So has everyone else in Writer's Club," I pointed out.

"Come on, what's the worst that could happen? Are you afraid I'll give you a bad review?"

"Why can't you just wait a few more weeks like everyone else?" I asked.

He leaned back in his chair and folded his arms across his broad chest. He scowled at me. I didn't like having him look that way.

"Because I don't believe you're really writing anything," he said after a long moment. "I don't think there's any long story except the one you've been telling about how you've been writing one."

"Why would I lie?"

"I don't know."

"I wouldn't. I haven't!" I stood and grabbed my package of crackers.

He looked up at me. "Show me. Let me help you."

"I don't *need* any help!"

I felt tears welling up in my eyes though, because The Poet had no idea what we were really talking about, and I did. I *did* need help—a lot of it! I turned and left the lunch room before the bell, and I locked myself in a bathroom stall.

Why wouldn't he leave me alone? Why did he have to be so cute and nice? I put my face into my hands and rocked and cried. I wished things were different. In another time, with another story, I'd be thrilled to hand over early pages for a critique, thrilled for his attentions. Even now, I wondered if there were any sections I could possibly give him that wouldn't be completely alarming to him. Maybe tonight I could look over the story and think about it. On the other hand, why risk it? Why give him any more time or attention?

Because I liked him. A lot. Two *L words*. I was losing control.

I wiped my eyes and went to the sink to repair my makeup. I still had afternoon classes to endure.

At the end of the day, I collapsed into the chair of my seventh period study hall, exhausted. I knew I needed to use the last hour for homework, but for the moment I folded my arms, put my head on my desk, and just closed my eyes. My head hurt. Thinking about equations seemed out of the question.

"Boyfriend troubles, huh?" a deep voice from behind me said.

"I don't have a boyfriend," I mumbled into my arms.

"Then who was that guy you were sitting with at lunch today?"

I turned around and glared at Lonnie. "He's just a friend from Writer's Club."

"Looks like he's interested in being more than just friends," Lonnie said.

I scowled. "It's not like that."

"You're sure about that?"

No, I wasn't—not after today's lunch. I thought about the thrill of hope that shot through me every morning when I approached the writer's corner to see if he'd written anything new for me, or that fluttering feeling in my stomach whenever I headed down the hall toward Gym and caught a glimpse of his face through the crowd.

"It's none of your business," I said.

"That's what I thought."

I turned to the front of the room and opened my Calculus book. Behind me, Lonnie snickered and went to the far table where the other guys played cards. I turned to a blank page in my notebook and began working problems. My goal was to work so many that nothing on the final would seem tricky or unfamiliar—which meant a lot of problems.

After school, I went to my follow-up appointment with Dr. Bentsen. He was our long-time family doctor, and I knew I had to be careful about what I said because he'd tell Mom and Dad.

He clicked through my chart on the computer. "Refresh my memory. How long's this been going on now?"

"I started having this burning pain in my stomach around the beginning of junior year. Just sometimes, and when I mentioned it to Mom, she told me to chew a couple of antacids."

"Did that help?"

"Sometimes."

He furrowed his brow and scrunched his excessively bushy eyebrows together. "But then your parents separated this summer and things got worse, correct?"

I nodded and stared at the medical poster on the wall. It showed the cardiovascular system and listed the symptoms of heart disease and warning signs of heart attack. I'd learned the names of all the major arteries and veins in my physiology class. I understood the chambers of the heart.

"You were throwing up blood, as I recall," he said.

"One time." That was pretty freaky. That's when I told my parents that I really thought I needed to go to the doctor—and they agreed.

"No blood in the stool? Black, red…"

"No. I don't know. I don't think so." I blushed. Who thought to look for stuff like that?

He tilted his head back to look at something on the screen. A pair of glasses hung around his neck.

I waited.

"So!" He slapped his hands on his thighs, and I jumped. "The endoscopy confirmed the presence of a small ulcer, and we started you on medication about a month ago. How are you feeling now?"

"A little better?"

"Is that a question?"

"I haven't noticed a lot of difference yet," I confessed. "I'm still having burning."

"Have you cut out caffeine and spicy foods? Tomato-based foods, too."

I thought about the pizza and spaghetti and gallons of tea that I drank. "Not really."

"Those kinds of foods can irritate your condition, so you need to avoid them. What about taking the antacid?"

"I take it when the pain gets really bad."

"You shouldn't wait that long. If you take it regularly, it can help prevent the pain."

"It tastes like chalk," I protested.

"Do it anyway." He looked at the chart some more. "You've lost weight, Kimberly. Are you eating?"

"Yes!"

"Be sure to eat more. Don't skip meals." He scowled at me.

I lowered my head. It felt like his eyes could drill into my skull like mind-reading radar. Lying to him was useless.

"Kimberly, I can't help you if you won't follow my orders."

I sighed. "It's just that I can't give up caffeine. I need to stay up late to study. I have a lot of pressure right now. Grades are important for getting into college."

"I hate to break it to you, kiddo, but the pressure in college is going to be even worse than what you're under now. You have to find a way to manage stress and your studies in a healthy way because there's a long road ahead of you, and you're not preparing properly for the trip."

He began typing into the computer.

"I'm going to change your medication," he said. "But I want you to do the other things, too. Eat regular meals, avoid spicy foods and caffeine, and take antacids—even if they taste bad."

"Okay," I mumbled.

He launched out of his chair and headed for the door. "See you in another six weeks, okay? Stop worrying so much about everything."

At home that evening, I gave Mom an edited version of my appointment, focusing on the medication change and follow-up appointment in six weeks. When she went to bed, I went to my room to continue studying for several more hours—without a No Doze or iced tea.

Around midnight, I picked up my story and read through the pages I'd written. The Poet thought I was lying about writing a story. He said he wanted to see proof. I knew he only said that to manipulate me, but still he'd goaded me enough that I really wanted to find something safe enough to share. He was right that it would help to have a critique, even though the story was incomplete.

Nothing about this story was "safe," though. My main character, her goal, the plot—it all pointed back to me. He would see through it. Could I convince him that it was fiction?

13. Approval

October 28

Snow fell overnight, covering the grass and pine trees with a dusting of white. The roads were wet but not icy when I drove to school that morning. Before going to first period English, I went to Writer's Club and put a copy of my pages into The Poet's folder. I stood there for a moment, biting my lip, not certain.

I wanted him to like my story—what was there so far, anyhow. I wanted him to tell me how to make it better, so that it would be perfect before I showed it to hyper-critical people like Dad.

I wanted to sit with him at lunch again.

In Honor's English class, Mr. Brown stroked his beard and asked, "Who can name a truly personal desire?"

"My own car," one of the guys said.

"You *think* that is a truly personal desire, but doesn't it also sneak in the delusion of prestige? The stamp of approval from others? *Nice car.*"

We stared at him. We knew he gave us trick questions.

"Love," someone else said.

"What people call 'love' is often a play for approval too, isn't it?" he asked. He paced in front of the classroom. "The trophy wife is the obvious one. The affair. Tabloids make millions on publishing who's dating whom. Even all the public displays of affection around here—who is the intended audience? Is it because of *true love*, or to make my friends gape at me?"

He stopped and looked around, smiling, smug.

"The dream to be an astronaut."

"Is this your dream, Gary?" Mr. Brown asked.

He glanced around the room before mumbling, "Yeah."

"Why do you want to be an astronaut?"

"To see things. To go where no one has gone before."

Mr. Brown raised his eyebrows. "A *Star Trek* fan?"

"Yeah." A shrug.

"Can you think of any family members who approve of your dream to become an astronaut, who think it's a prestigious thing?"

"My dad thinks it's totally cool," Gary said.

Mr. Brown nodded. "There it is again: approval. Is there really any truly personal desire, one not motivated or fueled somehow by the approval of another?"

"What's wrong with that, anyway?" someone asked.

"I'm not offering a value judgment," Mr. Brown said. "I'm just asking the questions. You tell me whether or not you think there's something wrong with it."

I thought about my dream to be valedictorian. Was it a truly personal desire? Was it mine, or was it motivated by the approval of others? The answer was easy. I wanted to be valedictorian to win scholarships—and also to have my dad boast about me to his friends, and my classmates recognize me. I wanted the prestige of being the winner.

But mostly I wanted to win scholarships.

"Isn't it better to be motivated by misplaced ambitions," I asked, "like pleasing your parents, than having no ambition at all?"

"Sure, I'm all for motivation, especially in students," Mr. Brown said. He began pacing again. "But, if you're only motivated by approval of others, you may find yourself very disappointed when you succeed."

I knew what he meant by that. One year I took the hunter's safety test and went deer hunting with Dad. I really thought I wanted to try it, and that he'd want me to go. But even though I shot a six-point buck, I felt no joy in the success. Whatever I'd expected Dad to say or do—he didn't.

"I don't think there's such a thing as a purely personal desire," someone else said. "Everyone works within the context of having parents, who influence their desires, and teachers and other mentors. No one lives in a vacuum."

The conversation continued. When the bell rang, I headed for Gym, hoping to see The Poet. The crowd of students in that hall seemed worse than normal, and I made my way to the side. The janitor's door loomed ahead of me, then beside me, but I passed without hyperventilating. I wondered where Tim was now. Was he at peace? Did he regret it?

The Poet was leaning against the wall. He wore a red tee shirt, his hands shoved into the front pockets of his jeans, his biceps bulging. His black hair was thick and wavy. Suddenly, his blue-green eyes locked on mine, even through the maze of people. He smiled and came toward me.

"Thank you," he said.

"For your eyes only. It's a pre-release copy, only for very special people."

"So I'm a very special person, am I?" he asked in a low voice.

I blushed. "I mean it."

"Cross my heart." He made the motion across his chest, never taking his eyes away from mine. "I'll read it during third period study hall."

I took a deep breath.

"Relax." He took my hand and squeezed. "I won't give you a bad review."

He was holding my hand!

"I know," I said.

"Sit with me again at lunch?"

I nodded, gulped.

"I'll have some comments for you by then." His eyes pinned me against the lockers.

"Okay," I breathed.

He released my hand. "I don't want to make you late for class."

I shook my head. "See you."

"Bye."

I hurried to Gym and changed clothes. I couldn't stop thinking about what happened, and every time the ball came to me, I messed up. What was I doing? I told him that I wasn't any good for him, to stay away, and now *this*!

The thought of his hand clasping mine made my cheeks heat up. For a moment I surrendered to the fantasy that we could be together. I gave up on valedictorian and college, and instead, we ran off to Broadway together, where he sang, wrote plays and poetry, acted, and I... I waited tables or something. Cleaned nasty apartments like my cousin's.

In Calculus, Mr. Underhill went over some new material that he wanted to include on the final. I took careful notes. I wished the test was only cumulative, a review, but nobody asked me about what was fair.

When I met Donna outside the cafeteria, The Poet was nowhere in sight. She noticed my looking.

"Is he joining us for lunch today?" she asked.

"I'm not sure." I bit my lip and looked at her with sheepish, squinted eyes. "We might sit by ourselves again."

"Oh, I see how it is!" Donna rolled her eyes dramatically and turned her back on me. "She has a boyfriend and suddenly forgets all about her best friend."

"He's not my boyfriend."

"Despite my copious wooing words," said a horribly familiar male voice from behind me.

I closed my eyes, feeling my cheeks begin to flame. I wanted to melt into the floor.

A warm hand fell on my shoulder and squeezed. He whispered in my ear, "Though I am persistent."

Donna half-turned toward us and smiled. "Hello again, Elliot." She handed a tray to him.

"Why, thank you, Donna."

I stepped forward into line without a tray.

"What are you doing for Halloween this year?" Donna asked him.

"I'm going to a party to see some friends of mine perform a few songs I wrote. Their band is pretty good. You guys want to come?"

"Can't, we're already going to another party," Donna said.

"Where Donna has a romantic interest," I pointed out.

"Ah." He nodded with understanding.

"I didn't know you wrote songs," I said.

"Lyrics. My friend writes the music."

"Bring them," I said. "I'd love to read them."

"Songs are meant to be heard."

I already knew that he could sing well. "I suppose you play an instrument, too?"

"Guitar and piano."

"So why don't you write your own music, too?" Donna asked.

"I'm not any good at it," he admitted. "I can play, but that's about it."

"So you're not planning to write any musicals on Broadway," I teased.

"Only as collaborative efforts."

We'd reached the part of the line where the rack of crackers and other snack foods were displayed. I grabbed my usual lunch.

"Why don't you eat real food?" he asked.

"This is real."

"It's junk. Buy some fruit or something."

"California." Donna rolled her eyes.

I ignored him and went to the cashier. I waited for them to go through the line. "Where do you want to sit?" I asked him.

"Follow me."

I looked at Donna for a moment. "Sorry," I mouthed. She waved me off.

The Poet was already a few tables away, and I hurried to catch up. He found an empty table along the wall. It wasn't near either of our usual groups. "A little privacy," he said. "As much as you can find in a school cafeteria, anyway."

I thought of him taking my hand in the hall earlier, and I grew warm. "What do we need privacy for?"

"Sit."

I sat. We stared at each other. He looked so freaking hot in that red tee-shirt.

"I read your pages." His expression was stern.

"Oh." Suddenly I understood. He wasn't mesmerized by me; he was repulsed. "That bad, huh?"

"It's all about you."

I shook my head. "No, I write fiction."

"A high school senior who wants to be valedictorian, but she's having trouble in one of her classes. Sounds a lot like you."

"It's the premise of the *story*. It's not a story about *me*, personally!"

"Okay, okay, don't be so defensive," he said. "It's fiction. Let's go with that then." He rolled his eyes.

I folded my arms across my chest and scowled.

"Great hook on page one," he said. "You pulled me right into the story from the first line, and you've created

Mandy's world in a very realistic way. In the few pages you've given me, I understand what she wants and what she's up against. She's funny and has a distinctive voice."

He paused and smiled. I blushed.

"But," he added, "the dialog with her parents is a little flat, and there isn't a lot of conflict. I think you could do more there. Also, her group of friends seem pretty one-dimensional. I can't really tell them apart."

"Okay, I can see that."

"How much do you have finished?"

"About two-thirds. I haven't written the ending yet."

"Let me have more pages," he said. "You didn't let me have very much."

I shook my head. I'd given him as many pages as possible without going into Mandy's thoughts of suicide. I knew he'd think the story was about me—which he did—so I couldn't let him read that part too. Not until finals were over, and I knew how the story ended.

"It's hard to give you a lot of feedback with just this." He pushed the pages across the table. He'd put some marks on things. I loved that. Some people hated to receive feedback, but I knew I had blind spots about my own writing. I couldn't see what was obvious to others. Critique helped so much.

"Thank you," I said.

"My brother's like your character, *Mandy*." He said her name with sarcastic emphasis. "Obsessed with grades, college, going somewhere with his life."

"You make that sound like a bad thing." I searched his face for clues.

"Toby's forgotten why he's doing any of it. He wanted to be an architect. That was his dream. But he listened to so many other people telling him what he needed to do with his life, and he got so caught up in trying to chase some idea about what 'going somewhere' meant, that now he's pursuing some medical research degree at Berkeley instead."

"Does he like it?"

"So far, he hates it. He's gained ten pounds since leaving for college, and he's depressed. I keep telling him to switch majors. Switch colleges. Change *something*. He's only a freshman, and there's plenty of time to change. Toby's not like that though. It's like he's made a decision, and now that he's on the course, he'll stay on it to the bitter end, even if it's the wrong course, even if he has the power to change it."

"Being driven is a positive quality," I pointed out.

"Driven people have heart attacks."

"They also run the world."

"Is that what's important to you?" He glared at me.

I shook my head. "I just want job security."

He laughed, but it wasn't a nice sound. "You and Toby can be valedictorians of your classes, and go to big-name colleges, and neither of you will have any more job security than I'll have in New York, trying to make it on Broadway. The idea of job security is an illusion."

"Education doesn't guarantee job security, but it definitely helps."

"That depends on what you want to do."

I could tell we would only fight on this subject. I looked down at the markups on my pages. "I guess I need to figure out what Mandy wants to be and include that in her career goal for college. That's not clear here."

"Or you could explore the angle of *why* she thinks she's supposed to go to college at all. Is it because someone's telling her to go? Society? A teacher?"

"She decided for herself. She's seen how hard it's been on her mother—single mother, raising her alone on a minimum-wage income. Mandy wants a different life for herself."

"Is the mother's hardship a lack of education?" he asked. "Or is it being a single mother with a low-wage job?"

"It all plays together, but she makes comments to Mandy about how she wishes she'd gone to college and chosen a career for herself."

He nodded. "Okay, so bring more pages and let me see. I'll tell you if it's playing out the way you want it to."

"I've shown you too much already."

"This hasn't helped you?"

I tucked my hair behind my ear and bit my lip. "Actually, it helps a lot."

"Then why won't you—"

"Because it's very dark, and I don't want you getting all weird about it."

"Since when am I weird about darkness? I told you that I love your dark work."

I stared at him. I didn't know what to do. I wanted to trust him but couldn't. Could I? I wanted to have more conversations like this, about even deeper subjects, but I was afraid he'd freak out and ruin everything.

But I liked him—a lot.

"Some might think it would be inappropriate to write a story about teen suicide after what happened with Tim," I said, thinking of Donna.

He gave me a sharp look. "Some would say it's therapeutic."

"Which side of the fence do *you* fall on?"

His eyes remained focused on my face. "I spent a few hours in the closet with you during the shooting. I would find it therapeutic."

I took a deep breath and exhaled slowly. "If I bring you more pages, you have to treat them like top-secret documents. Writer's Club might not be ready to handle a story like this. Or Mr. Brown."

"Do you want me to sign in blood or something?"

We stared at each other, silent.

"No, I just want you to keep your promise," I said.

"I will."

14. Accomplice

October 29

On Wednesday morning before class, I put a manila envelope with a full working copy of my story into The Poet's folder at Writer's Club. My hands shook. I stared at the filing cabinet. Everything was happening so fast. My physics final was two days away, and the Calculus final was on Monday. Then I'd know if these pages were really fact or fiction.

This was a terrible idea. I reached for the folder to take it back.

"Hey, thanks!" A familiar voice came from behind me.

I spun around. "What are you doing here?"

"The same thing you are." The Poet took the folder.

"I've changed my mind. Give that back."

The smile on his face vanished. "Really?"

He looked crestfallen. After another moment of hesitation, I dropped my hand and shrugged. "Aren't you ever nervous about showing your stuff?"

"Every time. Especially my songs, because they can be so personal."

I nodded. "Yeah, I can see that." I wrapped my arms around my middle.

He tipped his head to the side, and black bangs slid across his forehead. "But it's always worth it when I see someone enjoy something that I've created."

"What about when they hate it?"

"I get a kick out of that, too." He smiled again. The manila envelope rested in his hands. He held it out to me, questioning.

I shook my head. "Keep it. Just remember, this is an early, early draft. It will be way better when I'm done."

"I know."

"And it's dark."

"I like dark."

We walked down the hall together toward our first period classes. I barely made it to Mr. Brown's room before the bell. He was returning papers, and he handed mine to me when I slid into a seat. Across the top, he'd written, "98% A, Great Job!"

The class discussion topic was euthanasia— specifically, physician-assisted suicide and whether or not that should be allowed. Under what circumstances? Who decides? The conversation interested me a lot because obviously I supported suicide. Others in the class thought that life was sacred, even if the person was in a coma.

On the way to Gym, I saw The Poet in the hall. We smiled at each other, but he didn't leave his post by the wall. I saw my pages in his hand. He bent his head to let me know he was reading. That sent my heart pounding. I wondered what he thought so far. Maybe he'd have something to say at lunch.

In Calculus, Mr. Underhill went over the new material he'd introduced yesterday. I copied everything that he wrote on the board into my notebook. It no longer looked like ancient hieroglyphics, but I still became confused easily.

Our final was only a couple of days away now. I'd been studying every night—working problems over and over. I understood the material. The pressure came from needing a hundred percent on the final to earn an overall A for the grading period.

I could do it.

But if I didn't, was I really prepared to follow through with my plan?

Yes, I was pretty sure I could.

These thoughts seemed incredibly morbid to be having during high school Calculus class. I doubted that any of my classmates shared my black frame of mind. Looking at their faces, I saw the usual array of expressions—attention, boredom, sleepiness, distraction. Was I the only one who felt this way?

In Physics, Mrs. Lynch reminded us again about the final on Friday and what we could expect on the test. As with Calculus, I'd been studying and working problems; the stress came from requiring such a perfect score.

Donna met me outside the cafeteria before lunch. "You eating with *him* again today?"

"I don't know. Maybe."

"You're still going to the Halloween party this weekend, right?"

"Yes, I promised you that I would!"

She stuck out her lower lip. "I feel like I'm losing my best friend."

"Because I sat with him at lunch for the past two days?" I asked.

"Right now, it's just lunch. Then you'll start dating, and it'll be Friday nights, Saturday nights, and I'll never see you again."

"The same thing could happen with you and Jason."

"It could. Theoretically."

"But right now, neither of us is dating anyone," I pointed out.

"Right."

We stepped into line. She picked up a tray.

"My mom dropped a bombshell on me the other night," I said. "Apparently, the reason she left my dad is because he was having an affair."

"Shut your mouth!"

I shrugged. "That's what she said."

"Did you ask him about it?"

"*No*, I didn't ask him! What am I supposed to say? 'Hey Dad, I heard you're having an affair, is it true?'"

"Yeah, something like that."

"I'm not sure it's even any of my business."

"It's affected your life, hasn't it? Seems like that makes it your business."

"So what if it's true? What then? It doesn't change anything except make me even madder at him."

"At least you're not mad at *her* anymore for leaving. You can be mad at the right parent."

I rolled my eyes. "Yes, that's helpful."

"Ladies, hello," a familiar voice said from behind me.

"Hi, Elliot," Donna said in a falsetto voice. "Are you joining us for lunch today?"

"Actually…" He looked at me. "I was hoping to have Kim to myself again today so we could talk about her story."

I nodded. "Okay."

He put his tray on the railing beside me. "No lunch again?"

"These crackers constitute a healthy lunch of both protein—peanut butter—and carbohydrates."

He shook his head. "What about fruits and veggies?"

"I'm allergic," I quipped.

"To what?"

"Fruits and veggies."

"*All* of them?" He laughed.

"Yes."

"I think you're lying to me."

"Don't even go there," Donna warned him.

"Hmm."

We paid for our food, and then Donna headed toward our regular table with our friends. She waved goodbye. I followed The Poet to another table along the wall. Voices echoed and roared in the high-ceilinged lunchroom.

We sat down. He looked at me with those brilliant aquamarine eyes. I squirmed.

"What?" I finally asked.

"Your story's really good—a fast read."

I nodded. I didn't trust my voice.

"So, is she going to do it or not?" His eyes were intense.

"That's the whole story question. You'll just have to wait and see."

"Kim." His tone was kind. He took my hand, and I felt a lump rising in my throat. If he was too nice to me, I'd fall apart. I pulled away.

"I told you that it was fiction," I said.

"Really? You're just going to keep saying that?"

I studied the surface of the table. "You said that you could give me feedback. Talk about characterization, plotting, dialog."

"I've marked up the copy."

"Great, thanks."

I waited for him to slide the pages to me, but he didn't move. I looked up at him.

"I'm really worried about you," he said.

I stared at him. The lump felt thick, burning. I waited for it to shrink so I could speak.

"I remember when we were in the closet together," I said. "When Tim was shooting in the school, though we didn't know what was happening at the time. I remember feeling so scared. After I heard what happened, and our class talked about suicide, I thought a lot about Tim. What did he feel in those days and hours before he did what he did? What was he thinking? He didn't leave a note or anything, so we don't know."

He shook his head. "No, we don't."

"I wanted to write a story that showed what someone *might* be thinking and feeling, and what could lead a person to make such a decision. Does it come across? Have I succeeded?"

"Yes."

"Tell me. What does Mandy feel?"

For several silent seconds, his eyes penetrated mine, and when he began to speak, he never took his gaze off me. "Hopeless. She doesn't see any way out of her situation. She's lost control. She's constructed her whole identity around this ideal self—valedictorian—and she doesn't believe she can live with failure to achieve this goal. She's also depressed, clinically depressed, and needs professional help with that. Am I close?"

I nodded.

"But Mandy is *smart*," he added, "which means she's the kind of character that can learn and grow. She can experience failure and realize that it won't destroy her. She can seek help for depression and become whole. Her story doesn't have to end her life in tragedy."

"That's what you expect to happen, so maybe I'll do something else, just to shake it up."

"If she dies at the end, then the story hasn't been therapeutic or healing. She's only repeated Tim's mistake."

He assumed that Tim made a mistake. Not me.

"I warned you that it's dark," I said quietly.

He reached into his back pocket and threw a wad of papers onto the table. It was the story, folded lengthwise and slightly rolled, curling and dog-eared.

"I don't know what I'm supposed to do with this," he said. "I should talk to Mr. Brown or something."

My eyes flew open in horror. "No! You can't!"

"You wouldn't be so secretive about it if this were just a story."

I leaned forward and hissed, "You *promised* you wouldn't tell anyone!"

"You shouldn't have put me in this position."

"*You* were the one who insisted on seeing the pages," I pointed out.

"But what if you—"

"Look, I'm not your responsibility." I tucked a strand of hair behind my ear and tried to control my voice. "You don't have to worry or—"

"I *am* worried! I *do* have a responsibility. You've given me a pre-suicide note to read, and now you're telling me to pretend that it's just fiction. Do you know how messed up that is?"

"I'm sorry I trusted you."

He raked a hand through his black hair. "You can trust me. I keep my promises. But I want you to make a promise to me, too."

"What?" I eyed him warily.

"Call me. Before you do it, if you're even thinking about it, call me first."

"Elliot's Suicide Hotline Prevention?" Saying his name out loud gave me a rush.

"Something like that. Just promise, will you?" He took out a pen and wrote his number across the top of my chapter. He underlined it. "Okay?"

I bit my lip. I didn't want to make this kind of promise. What was I supposed to say? *Hi Elliot, I'm going to kill myself now and just wanted to say goodbye. Don't bother trying to talk me out of it. I kept my promise.*

"Okay?" He raised his eyebrows, expecting an answer.

"Sure, whatever."

"That's a promise. I'm keeping mine. You keep yours." He slid the pages across the table to me. "I hope these help."

"Thanks." I shuffled through a few. He'd given me some good detailed comments, like before, the kind that I'd hoped to see. I wanted to break the tension of our conversation, so I added, "That's a pretty convoluted way to give a girl your phone number."

The edges of his lips curled up the smallest bit. "You don't respond well to sappy love poems, so I thought I'd try a different route."

"So... tell me more about this band of yours," I said.

"It's not really *my band*," he said. "They play some of my songs, but otherwise that's it."

"Are you friends with any of them?"

"I met the lead vocalist over the summer, and we've hung out a little. They're older, in their twenties, so they go to clubs and stuff a lot."

"Are you a groupie?" I joked.

He smiled. "No. They're not that good."

"You'd better eat some of that." I pointed at his lunch tray. "The lunch period's almost over. Mine's portable. One of the many virtues of peanut butter crackers."

"I've lost my appetite."

"I'm sorry."

He reached under the table and took my hand. "When are your finals?"

"Physics is Friday, and Calculus is Monday."

"You ready?" He squeezed.

"Yeah, I think so. As ready as I can possibly be. I've been studying my butt off."

We looked at each other. I felt relieved that he'd agreed to keep my secret about the story. Elliot looked like he wanted to say something else, but he didn't. We just sat there, holding hands, surrounded by the roar of the lunchroom, staring at one another until the bell.

15. All Hallows

October 31

On Friday night after school, Donna came over, and we hung out for a couple of hours at the trailer. She repainted her toenails. They were long and perfect, like her fingernails, and she could scrunch up her toes in a funny pose. My jointless little toes didn't bend that way. We laughed about my feet. We laughed about everything. With my Krazy Kim mask, Donna had no clue about my dark secrets or what I was really feeling and planning.

While we were getting ready to leave for the Halloween party, I said, "Tonight's the night for you and Jason. I'm psychic. I can see it." I blotted my lipstick with a tissue.

"He probably won't even come." She ran a brush through her hair one last time. She stuck her tongue out at the mirror.

I bumped her shoulder with mine. "He will. And you're going to be more than *coy* this time."

"I don't know what to say to him."

"Just be yourself. You ready?"

The party was in the basement of a guy's house. No one dressed up in costumes, but they hung some orange colored lights and plastic spiders from the ceiling. Loud music played. Jason handed Donna and me a couple of wine coolers from a blue ice chest. I could see why she liked him; he was a cute guy, tan, with an angular jawline and dark brown hair that he brushed carefully into tousled waves away from his face. He was two inches shorter than she was.

We sat at one of the card tables and played poker for awhile. Our friend Bob showed up. He wore a red bandana around his head, a black leather jacket, jeans, and heavy black work boots. He was a biker and one of the voc-tech kids, specializing in mechanical and automotive. He looked like he could lift a car, not just fix one, but he was one of the sweetest guys in school. He'd do anything to help anyone.

"Can I have some of that?" I asked, pointing at the bottle of vodka in his hands.

"I brought it just for you," he said with a wink. "I know you hate beer." He poured about a fourth of the bottle over ice into a plastic red cup and handed it to me.

Donna gave me a look. "No mixer?"

"I forgot the cranberry and orange juice," Bob said, laughing.

I took a sip and winced. "Don't worry, I'll drink slowly."

Donna shook her head. "I'm not carrying you out of here tonight."

I looked at Bob. "I'll carry her," he said cheerfully before someone pulled him outside to look at their new truck.

Jason sat close beside Donna at the card table. They put their heads together, whispering, whispering, and Donna smiled with joy. Though I was happy for her, I felt left out because I didn't know anyone besides her and Bob. Feeling shy, I drank straight vodka and stared at my cards.

I wished that I was with Elliot tonight instead of here.

Donna lit another cigarette and shuffled the deck for the next game. The cards purred between her fingers. When Bob returned to the table and asked Donna for a cigarette, Jason said to him, "Bet you can't drink the whole thing." He gestured toward the fifth of vodka that Bob was drinking straight from the bottle.

"How much?"

"Twenty."

"Fifty," Bob said.

"I don't have fifty."

Someone else pulled out their wallet. "I have fifty. Let's see it."

Bob eyed the money on the table for a moment, and then he rolled up the sleeves of his blue and black checkered flannel shirt. He raised the bottle to his lips. He drank and drank and actually drained the rest of the fifth. He wiped his lips with his left forearm and grinned at us. "I'll take your fifty dollars."

"You're a maniac."

"You're going to throw up."

Bob took the money and shrugged. No one said he had to *keep* it down, only that he had to *get* it down.

We played more cards. I smiled and kept quiet, watching others in the room. Donna neglected me, but I didn't hold it against her. She kept blushing at things Jason said. An hour and a half passed, maybe more. I began feeling more and more lonely and depressed. My head began to swim, and I could barely read my own cards. My cheeks went numb. I reached for my glass again but had trouble grasping it.

"Maybe you ought to quit for awhile," Donna said to me.

"Okay."

She could have told me to jump off a bridge, and I would have said okay. In fact, jumping off a bridge sounded like a great idea. I stood up from the table. All the cigarette smoke was starting to burn my eyes and make my head hurt.

"Where are you going?" she asked.

"I don't want to play anymore."

"You all right?" Jason and the others at the table looked at me, too. I hated having all those people staring like I was some kind of freak.

"Uh-huh."

Bob had already gone outside to throw up. I felt sick, too. Donna and Jason exchanged glances like they thought that's where I was heading. I didn't care what they thought.

The next thing I remembered was lying in the back seat of Donna's Honda, sobbing. I didn't know how I ended up there. I must have blacked out. Bob was in the front seat, asking me what was wrong, looking panicked.

"I wish I was *dead*!" I cried.

"Aw, Kim, no you don't. Whatever it is, it ain't that bad."

"I *failed*! It's all over. It's *hopeless*!" Tears streamed down my face, soaking my shirt and the seat. I couldn't stop crying.

"What's hopeless?" He wrapped his arms around the headrests and stared at me.

"My life is over. I failed. *I failed!*" I couldn't stop crying. I curled into a ball, hugging my stomach, sobbing.

"I'm going to find Donna, okay? Don't do anything, okay?"

I rocked. That's all I could manage. I bawled and rocked. My buzzing head spun crazily. Drinking all that vodka had been a bad idea. After several minutes, Bob returned with Donna. The overhead light came on as she climbed into the car.

"Kim? What's wrong?" Her voice was kind and concerned.

"I failed, I failed, I failed." I moaned and covered my face. "I'm a big fat failure!"

"How did you fail?"

"I should have studied more."

She didn't say anything for a moment. Then she asked, "Did you goof around? Were you up all night playing video games and stuff?"

"No."

"No," she agreed. "As I remember, you stayed up all night studying, a lot. You went without sleep to study. You did everything you could."

"But it wasn't enough. I still failed." I sniffled and took a deep breath. "I'm probably not going to get straight A's."

"Big deal, neither am I."

"But it doesn't *matter* to you!" I cried. "It means *everything* to me!"

"Why? Why does it matter so much?"

"Because I want to be valedictorian." Each word came out as a blubbery sob.

"That doesn't answer the question," Donna said. "Why do you want to be valedictorian? Why is that so important to you?"

I could tell by the sound of her voice that she was impatient with me. Depressed Kim was no fun. We were at a party, and I was ruining everything. I felt bad, but I couldn't help it. My head kept spinning and spinning, and the crying wouldn't go away. I felt completely out of control.

"To go to college, to win scholarships," I said. "You already know all that!"

"No," Donna said. She stared at me. "It's something more than that. You can find a way to go to college without being valedictorian. Plenty of kids do. So what is it? What's *really* driving you?"

I stared at the blackness beneath the driver's side seat. "I don't know," I whispered.

"Well, don't you think you'd better figure that out?"

"I just want to win," I said meekly. "I want to beat the cliques, the rich kids."

"This is *not* about Heidi Jones," Donna said scornfully. "If you're out here bawling and scaring poor old Bob by saying you wish you were dead, and it's all because you are going to lose class rank to Heidi Jones, I'll kill you myself. I swear."

I sniffled.

"Suicide isn't something to joke about," Donna said. "Bob and Tim Maiers were *friends*. He's super freaked out right now because of what you said. It hasn't even been a month since Tim's funeral."

I wanted to talk to Donna. She was supposed to be my best friend. But I knew that talking would only make things worse. I was on my own now.

"I'm sorry," I said. "I've ruined everything again. Epic fail."

Donna sighed. "You might be a giant woobie with a serious case of cranium rectumitis right now, but you're *not a failure*. Hear me?"

I nodded.

"Jason is in there, *talking* to me. Do you know how long I've waited for this to happen?"

"Go back inside. I'm fine."

"You're not fine. Obviously. I have to take you home."

"No, no. You go back and flirt with Jason. Send Bob out here to talk to me."

"Bob's throwing up. He's no good to anyone."

"I'm no good to anyone either."

"Shut up." She opened the car door.

"Where are you going?"

"For my jacket and keys."

"No, we don't have to go! Jason is talking to you."

"He'll talk to me another time."

"I'm sorry. I will never drink straight vodka again. Very bad idea."

"You think?" She slammed the door. My head buzzed and spun in an alarming way. I knew I'd be very sick in the morning. I'd probably throw up on the way home. I pressed my face against the cold vinyl seat and stared into the blackness. I was no good for anybody. I just wanted it all to stop. I wanted it to be over.

16. Adversity

November 3

On Monday morning, I sat at my desk in Calculus class. Sleet tapped against the windows. Muddy ditches in front of the school overflowed their banks, and the gray sky seemed to hover just inches above the treetops. Voices of other kids murmured around me. I was ready for the test. I'd studied hard but also knew from past experience that didn't mean much.

To earn an overall A in the class, I needed a perfect score on the final. One hundred percent.

Mr. Underhill dashed into the classroom, shirt untucked in the back, wild sprigs of gray hair flying, and threw a handful of folders onto the center of his desk. "Sorry I'm late," he said. "Here, take one and pass it back."

Papers rustled through the rows. Panicked, I stared at the page for several seconds. My whole body shook. Everything came down to this one moment: my whole life.

No pressure or anything.

I took a deep breath and read the first problem. I knew what to do. The next one made sense too, and the one after that. With each problem, I felt more confident.

The very last problem was worth 10 points and was almost an exact replica of one of the homework problems. I'd worked this one a half dozen times on Sunday afternoon. It was hard. I didn't really understand it, but I'd memorized the steps. Now the solution wouldn't come to me. My thoughts raced—nervous and panicked—and butterflies churned in my stomach. I held my breath. Rain ticked against the window. Someone coughed in the back row.

Heidi Jones was the first to take her paper up and put it on Mr. Underhill's desk. Others began to follow. My last problem remained blank. I had to try something. I didn't even know where to start. I felt stupid and frustrated.

The bell rang. I hadn't put anything beneath the question. I dropped my test off with the others and walked to my third period class. My books felt like heavy stones. Streams of students filled the hallway and carried me along in their current. A rushing sound filled my ears. My hands were cold.

In Physics, Mrs. Lynch returned our graded final exams from Friday. Although I had answered the 10-point extra credit question correctly, I still fell 7 points short of the A. The pressure inside my lungs became suffocating. It was all over. Even without knowing how I did on the Calculus final, I only scored a B in Physics for sure. Since I didn't complete that last problem, I scored at least a B in Calculus, maybe worse.

After going over some of the problems in the exam, Mrs. Lynch began lecturing on a new chapter. I couldn't pay attention. What was the point? I had no more chances to fix it. I would not have straight A's. I would not be valedictorian. I wouldn't be able to go to college—at least not a *good* college, and certainly not a private university. My life was over.

No one could know, not yet. I had to pretend everything was okay. Just for a little while longer.

I met Donna outside the cafeteria after Physics. My stomach grumbled and burned. We hadn't talked *at all* about what happened at the party. The following morning after we woke up, she didn't hang out at my house long because she had to be at her grandmother's house at noon.

Now, I was afraid that she'd read the truth on my face about this morning's Calculus and Physics classes and realize my plans were real.

I tried to joke around as usual. "Anything happen with Jason today?" I asked.

"He was out sick. It was a sad day." She poked out her lower lip.

"Poor you."

"And poor Jason," she pointed out.

"Yeah, my sympathy goes out to him."

Elliot walked up to us. "Hey." He looked delicious wearing all black, very broad and muscular, and his dark clothes made the color of his aquamarine eyes more prominent.

"She's sitting with me today," Donna told him. "We have some things to discuss."

"Oh, well—is everything okay?" He glanced at me, concerned.

"Fine. She's jealous that you're getting so much of my attention," I said.

"And you haven't even asked her out on a date yet," Donna said.

"Donna!" I gave her a sharp elbow.

He grinned. "If that's the problem…"

My face flamed. "Please, just go. It's a girl thing."

He raised his hands in the air and backed away. "I don't want to be in the middle of *that*. Tomorrow then."

Donna and I stepped into the lunch line. She grabbed a lunch tray. I picked one up too. My stomach burned, and macaroni and cheese was on the menu.

She looked at my hands. "Wasn't your Calculus final this morning?"

I nodded, surprised that she remembered. She didn't usually pay much attention to my academic drama.

"So how'd you do?" she asked.

I shrugged and answered as honestly as I could. "I felt really good about everything except the last question."

"Think you scored an A?"

"Maybe…" If everyone else in the class missed at least one question.

She stared at the ground. It was a bad sign. She meant to have some kind of "talk" with me.

"Donna," I said before she could launch into a speech, "I was annihilated Friday night. I honestly don't remember half of what I said, but the parts that I do remember are humiliating. Please, please, please forget them. I was stupid. I was out of my mind."

"We used to talk, you know. You used to tell me everything."

"That was before things became so depressing. I know you don't like to listen to me when I'm in the dumps, and I've been depressed too much this fall, with my parents and my grades and everything else, and you've listened to my grumblings way more than a best friend should have to listen."

"That's what best friends *do*," she said.

"I wish I could tell you the whole story, but things are so complicated this time. I feel like I'm having a nervous breakdown or something—seriously."

"Should I call the men in white coats for you?" She smiled and winked.

"I'm not joking."

"You're not having a nervous breakdown, Kim, whatever you think." She slid her tray forward. I looked around, but no one was listening to our strange conversation. "You're just stressed out and living too much in your head because you're not talking to me or anyone else."

"I feel like I don't know how to talk anymore," I mumbled. "Everything is blocked inside my head by a gray curtain."

"Apparently I just need to take you out and get you wasted. Then you'll blather on and on to anyone who'll listen—like poor Bob. He was so upset."

I blushed. "I'm so sorry about that. Again, sorry. Humiliation. I'll talk to him."

We shuffled in silence. Then she asked, "Can you try to describe what you're going through?"

I took a moment to think. What was safe to say?

"I'm just not *me* anymore," I began. I watched her face, and she nodded, expectantly. "Like the other weekend, when you and I read all those old notes of ours, it felt like the first time in months that I'd truly laughed with you, instead of faking it. I wish I could go back to being happy all the time—the old sunny, smiley, giggly Kim I used to be. I don't know what happened to me. I don't know who I am anymore, but I don't like the new me. I feel like I have to hide my real feelings all the time, and I end up feeling all fake, on the outside looking in."

"Why do you feel like you have to hide?" she asked.

"Because no one will like the person I've become."

We were almost to the cashier. "Who is that?" Donna asked.

I took a deep breath and blurted out, "The one who kept saying, 'I'm a failure. I don't want to live.' The one you met Friday night."

"Oh."

Oh. See? She didn't want to know the whole truth. It was ugly.

I spotted Elliot sitting with his friends in the middle of the cafeteria. The truth was that I didn't know what I wanted, not really. Sometimes I wanted to die. Sometimes I wanted to be alive and happy and in love. More than anything, I just wanted to stop feeling so bad all the time.

Donna saw the direction of my gaze. "So live for love, like the rest of us. Live for The Poet."

"He's going to New York after graduation to be on Broadway," I said. "We don't have the same goals in life. I don't think there's a future for us."

"People change."

"The only person I can depend on is myself," I said. "Me, myself, and I, and I need to earn straight A's, and go to college, and take control of my own destiny. Love would be great, but I can't control love. I can't control the other person and whether or not we'll go in the same direction."

I handed one of my tickets to the cashier, blushing. Donna looked away. She knew how much I hated being different this way. She ought to realize this was a perfect example of why I needed to be valedictorian, to win, to change my future, to be a success.

Donna paid for her lunch with cash, and then we started toward the table where our friends sat.

"We should talk like this more," Donna said.

"Yeah." I plastered a false smile on my face. "I'd like that."

"Guess what?" Bobbi said as we sat. "I bought the tickets!"

"For what?" I asked.

"Kim, have you not been paying attention to anything the past two weeks?" Donna asked.

"I've been kind of *stressed out* by *finals*!" I said.

"To see Bon Jovi!" Bobbi said.

"Oh, *that*! Congratulations." I smiled. "Are they good seats?"

"On the floor!"

Everyone started talking about their favorite bands and concerts. I ate my lunch and only half listened. It was just another day for everyone else, but all I could think about was that letter written in permanent ink in Mrs. Lynch's grade book: B, Physics.

In one week, report cards would come out. In one week, everyone would know that I was a failure. In one week, I was going to die.

17. Actress

November 4

When the alarm went off on Tuesday morning, I awoke with a feeling of lightness, which seemed strange, considering. Then I realized the reason: no more worrying, despairing, stressing, and struggling. Now I knew how the story ended. I felt a tremendous sense of peace, just knowing.

In one week, on November 10, report cards would come out. That would be my last day.

That was the deadline to finish writing my story.

I went to the kitchen, fed Boots, and ate cereal for breakfast. Outside, cold drizzle turned the world into a gray, foggy place, but for once the rain didn't dampen my good mood. I turned up the radio and sang the whole way to school. On my way to first period Honor's English class, I checked the writer's corner. Elliot had left a new poem.

Floozy
Betty Sue lost her red bootie
beside the red tattooed
man when she left the Jacuzzi.

You can bet your sweet patootie
she also forgot to
inform him about her cooties.

I snickered and covered my mouth. Short and to the point. I loved it.

I grabbed some blank comment sheets and headed to Mr. Brown's classroom. I slid into my seat just before the bell. Mr. Brown walked to the front of the class and began talking. His reddish-brown hair, beard, and mustache looked newly trimmed, shorter than usual, and it made him seem even younger. He pushed his dark framed glasses up with a finger.

"If you could murder someone and get away with it," Mr. Brown began, "would you do it?"

What a question.

He brought his hands together in prayer position beneath his chin and raised his eyebrows. "Anyone want to start?"

"No, it's wrong to kill someone, no matter what," Heidi said.

Brown-noser.

"Some people are bad and deserve to die," another said.

"Are there 'good people' and 'bad people'?" Mr. Brown asked.

I thought about him sitting at home every night, devising questions like this to torment us with during first period. Early in the school year, he told us that his job as an educator was to teach us how to *think*. Think about hard questions and write five-paragraph essays every day.

"People are fundamentally good," someone said. "You can find good in almost everyone."

"Even the rapist? The child molester? The murderer?" Mr. Brown asked.

"Just because they've done bad things doesn't make them bad *people*."

"Maybe your ideas are romantic and idealistic because of your youth," Mr. Brown said.

"Maybe you're a cynic because of your age," I pointed out, knowing full well that he was, at most, ten years older than we were.

"I'm a realist," he said. "I've seen more of the world than you, and I know there are seriously bad people—evil people."

"So would *you* murder someone if you could?" someone asked him.

"Wouldn't *you* like to know?" Mr. Brown dodged.

"Yes!" We all demanded.

"I would not," he said.

"Why not?"

"Someone else answer," he said. "If you wouldn't murder, even though you could, why not? Help me out here."

"Two wrongs don't make a right," someone said.

"A cliché, but you're on to something," Mr. Brown said. "Go on."

The discussion continued. At the end of the class, Mr. Brown returned our final papers. I'd written on Theodore Dreiser's *Sister Carrie*.

"See me after class," he said, placing the paper face down on my desk.

For a moment, I was too scared to look. What if I'd somehow bombed my final paper?

But this was Honor's English, my best class, and how could I have messed up? Well, given how the rest of this grading period had been going for me, anything was possible.

I flipped the paper. 100 percent, A.

I sighed with relief, then frowned. So why did he want to talk to me? This meant I'd miss seeing Elliot before Gym—an encounter I'd come to enjoy every day. At least I'd see him for sure in Writer's Club, and probably at lunch too.

What if Elliot had told Mr. Brown about my story? What if he hadn't kept his promise? He'd been pretty upset when he returned the last set of pages to me.

After the other students left, I approached Mr. Brown's desk cautiously. "You wanted to talk to me?"

"You liked this novel a lot," he observed.

I nodded. "I don't usually like classic literature, but this was a great story, and at the same time it had an important theme. It was really good."

"Your report was outstanding," he said. "The best in class, by far. If anyone else had turned in that paper, I'd wonder about cheating."

"You think—"

"No, I know it's your work. It's very, very good work."

"So…why did you want to talk to me?" I bit my lip, worrying again about what Elliot might have told him.

He leaned back in his chair and made an A-frame with his hands beneath his chin. He regarded me intently for several seconds. "Is everything okay, Kim?"

"Yeah." I nodded, swallowed, and looked at the floor. "Why?"

"You haven't turned any creative writing into Writer's Club for a month or so."

Uh-oh. Here it comes... I lifted my chin. "I'm working on a new story."

"Good. I was afraid you'd quit writing."

"No way. I love writing."

He stared at me. I was afraid that he'd ask me to talk about the new story—or worse, that he already knew everything. Keeping secrets had never been a strong suit of mine. My blushing face gave everything away.

"Have you thought about writing programs in college?" he asked.

"Sure, I've daydreamed about it, but I'll major in something like medicine or law or engineering—a career that makes money. I'm against poverty, you know."

He laughed. "Not all writers are poor, Kim. Look around you. The world is full of text that someone wrote as part of their job. There are plenty of professions that need good writers—journalism, teaching, marketing, technical writing and editing, literary agents... You can earn a living as a writer. You just might not start out as a best-selling novelist."

I thought about Dad's opinions on the matter. "My dad would have a stroke if I wasted my college education on something like writing."

Mr. Brown's eyebrows shot toward his receding hairline, and his eyes rounded. "*Wasted*, really?"

"His words, not mine."

"You might have just given me another class discussion topic—the value of a liberal arts education." He shook his head. "How are you doing with your situation with your parents these days?"

I wondered if he remembered this kind of detail on all his students' personal lives. Why was I under the microscope? "Fine."

He pursed his lips and nodded. "Mmm hmm."

"What?"

"Nothing, that's all. You're free to go."

I frowned but didn't need to be told twice. I hurried to Gym, barely making it before the bell.

In Calculus, Mr. Underhill returned our final exams. I scored a B. That meant I scored a B in the class overall, for sure. It was official: I was no longer valedictorian of the senior class. I had lost to Heidi Jones and probably to Tricia Cline as well. I probably couldn't go to college since I wouldn't be able to win an academic scholarship, and my whole future was ruined. I'd be stuck in this small town, a nobody with a dead-end job, doing nothing special.

Certainly not writing.

However, now I had to be prepared to lie to Donna and Elliot, if either of them asked, so that they wouldn't be suspicious about my intentions. I had one week left to live. One week until I saw the hard evidence and knew for sure, and then I couldn't have anyone stop me.

I met Donna outside the cafeteria. "There's a substitute for Mrs. Lynch today," I said. "He's not bad in the looks department."

"Oh, goody! I have Lynch for fifth period study hall."

"He didn't know a lot about Physics."

She tsked and picked some lint from her black sweater. "Well, it must be hard to come into the middle of a senior-level class like that and teach a lesson cold."

"When did you become so compassionate and understanding?"

"Love softens the pessimist's heart."

"Love, is it?" I snickered.

She leaned closer to me and whispered, "Jason asked me on a date."

"What? Tell everything. Now!"

"Shh!"

"Now!" I hissed.

"He asked if I wanted to go out to dinner with him Friday night, and I said yes. That's all."

"That's *all*? That's a *real* date. That's huge!"

Elliot bumped into me. "What's huge?"

I looked at Donna and raised my eyebrows. "It's your news to tell."

"I have a date."

"Who's the lucky guy?" Elliot asked.

"Maybe I'll let you meet him sometime." Donna turned and picked up a tray. "Who knows, we could double sometime or something." She winked at me.

I wanted to melt into the floor. My face heated up.

"You're adorable when you blush," Elliot said.

I put my hands to my face and moaned. He chuckled.

"Stop staring, you're making it worse," I said. "I hate being a redhead."

He twisted his fingers around mine and tugged me forward. "Come on, Red. Line's moving."

"How was the band?" I asked, trying to change the subject so my cheeks would cool off. "Did your music sound good?"

"It was awesome. I wish you could have been there. They even tried a new one that I hadn't heard them practice before. It sounded pretty good."

The warmth of his hand around mine felt searing and disorienting. We were in the middle of a crowded lunch room. "If they play clubs, how do you get in?" I asked. "I thought you had to be twenty-one."

He gave me a sheepish smile. "You do. Wes gives me a special band pass."

"Do you drink, too?"

"No, I just go for the music."

I nodded. "Makes sense. You can drink anywhere."

"Say, how was the Halloween party you went to?"

Donna looked over her shoulder at us and smirked. I stuck out my tongue. "I'm never drinking again," I said.

"That bad, huh?"

"Worse."

He released my hand to reach for one of the lunch entrees. "It happens to the best of us, I'm afraid."

"You?" I asked.

"Sure. Back in California, beach party, bonfire, tequila."

"Did you wake up with sand in your underwear?"

"I refuse to answer that question."

I laughed. "I have an image of you in a Jacuzzi with Betty Sue, the floozy who lost her red bootie."

He smiled, and his eyes danced. "I don't kiss and tell."

"This sounds intriguing," Donna commented.

"Elliot's poem for today." I recited the verses from memory.

"Wow," he said. "I'm flattered."

"I loved it," I said.

"You're blushing again."

"I do that a lot." I grabbed a package of crackers from the rack. He frowned.

We paid at the cashier, and then the three of us looked at each other. "I could sit with you guys today," Elliot ventured.

"Sure, that would be great," I said. "I'll introduce you to everyone."

We went to our table. All my friends wanted to talk to him, so I just sat and listened. The lunch period passed quickly. "See you at Writer's Club," he said before we headed our separate ways.

I went through my afternoon classes without adventure. I didn't pay much attention; instead, I replayed conversations with Elliot in my head. In last-period study hall, doing homework seemed like a total waste of time since my grades no longer mattered. In one week, I'd be dead.

Reality slammed into me. My mood plummeted. It really wasn't fair of me to flirt with Elliot and pretend that we had any kind of future together. Every minute that we spent together was an unkindness. It was too late for us.

I'd promised to call him before doing anything. Would I? What would I say? Goodbye, I supposed.

These thoughts felt unbearable. I put my head on my desk and closed my eyes. A few tears squeezed through my lids. My throat suddenly burned, raw.

Lonnie tapped me on the shoulder.

"Go away," I mumbled into my sleeve.

"What's up?"

"Tired."

"Come play cards with us," he coaxed.

"I don't want to."

"Look at me."

I lifted my head and turned to scowl at him.

"What's wrong?" he asked.

I opened my mouth, then shut it again. We stared at one another for several seconds.

Lonnie smiled. "You know, you didn't actually say anything just now."

The words seemed trapped inside my windpipe, unable to climb out of my mouth.

When I still didn't answer, his smile dropped. "Are you all right? You're not having a stroke or something, are you?"

I shook my head. "I…no. I didn't, I mean, I scored B's. In Calculus and Physics."

He looked at me, waiting. That obviously wasn't enough information for him.

"Not A's," I clarified.

"Not C's, or D's either," he pointed out. "I would have failed calculus. As in F."

"I…but that means that I'm no longer valedictorian," I explained. "I'm no longer number one."

"Who is? No! Don't say it—"

I nodded. "Heidi Jones."

He held his giant fists to the sky and grimaced as if to curse the gods. I smiled. He grinned back at me.

"It's not the end of the world, you know," he said. "So, are you number two now?"

"Number four."

"Out of how many?"

"Two hundred and thirty-seven."

"Pretty impressive." He stuck out his lower lip and nodded. "I'm probably one hundred and thirty-seven."

I couldn't believe I'd said it out loud. I wasn't valedictorian anymore. "This wasn't supposed to happen," I said. "I tried *so hard*. And now everything I've worked for all these years is just gone."

"Stuff happens. You can't always control it."

I didn't know why I was talking to him about any of this.

"It *feels like* the end of the world," I admitted. "Like my life is over."

He narrowed his eyes. "That's crazy talk, girl."

"Maybe I am crazy."

"So what? Now you don't have to give some big speech. Doesn't seem like such a bad thing to me." He shrugged with a cute, sleepy-eyed grin.

"Maybe I *like* giving big speeches."

"Do you?"

"No."

"Okay then. Come play cards with us. We'll cheer you up."

I hesitated.

"Come on," he urged. "I *know* you're not going to do any studying today."

So I went to the back table and let Lonnie deal me into the poker game with the guys. They were friends with

Bob and others at the Halloween party, and everyone had heard about me throwing up in the rhododendron bushes on my way to the car—which I only vaguely remembered doing. One of them played cards with me and Donna in the basement, and he told stories about how wasted I'd been, drinking straight vodka. Even I laughed at some of the ridiculous things I'd said.

As always, Mrs. Piper crocheted behind her desk. It was easy to forget she was even there. The pleasant smell of paint and turpentine hung in the air. A pair of worn brown work boots rested on a white sheet on the counter. A spotlight emphasized the shadows in the deep creases of the old leather. Frayed shoelaces curled in playful loops. Pencil drawings of this still-life hung around the room. I would have loved to join the other art students on this project, but instead, I now spent each morning in the science hall, surrounded by the stench of formaldehyde.

A lot of good that choice had done me.

When the bell rang, I stood.

"Kim, do you have a minute?" Mrs. Piper asked.

Another teacher keeping me after class—on the same day! I went to her desk. She stood and closed the door behind the last student. I avoided getting into trouble, and I could tell right away that I'd done something wrong. My cheeks burned. What did she want to talk to me about?

"Let's sit down," she said.

She sat close beside me at one of the big tables. Its surface was etched from knife slips and stained by ink and paint.

"I couldn't help overhearing you and your friends talking," she said. "I'm very concerned about you, Kim."

How long had she been listening? What had I said? I scanned the wide racks of flat shelves behind her shoulder, avoiding eye contact and stalling, but nothing came to mind. "I'm fine."

"Actually, I think you might have a drinking problem."

"What? No, I—we were just talking about a stupid party!"

"It sounds like you've been going to a lot of parties lately."

A lot? I'd been to maybe four or five parties all year. Maybe six. That wasn't a lot. But could she have me arrested for underage drinking? Why had she singled me out, but not the other boys who were also talking about the party? It wasn't fair! I didn't have a problem; all the other kids were drinking too, not just me. Me and my big mouth. Stupid, stupid!

She pinned me with pale blue eyes. "Several of your teachers have noticed what a hard time you're having this year. I know your parents separated over the summer."

I nodded, looked away again, and tried to swallow the unexpected marble in my throat. People noticed? My eyes burned.

"Do you want to talk about anything, Kim?" she asked.

"No!" I choked, shaking my head for added emphasis. Which other teachers had been talking about me in the lounge? Mr. Brown. Did all of them know about my personal life? How humiliating!

Then she started telling me about her own son, about his teenage drinking and his fatal car accident, and she cried.

Alcohol ruined lives, she said. Her voice was very caring and kind and sad. I felt awful for her family and insisted that I never drank while driving. Donna did all the driving.

After awhile, she blew her nose and wrote another pass for me. "I want you to make an appointment to talk to the school counselor."

Keeping my head lowered, I took the piece of paper and left. There was no way I was going to talk to anyone on the faculty about what was really going on in my life. Obviously, they all gossiped about students in the lounge. My secrets wouldn't be safe.

Despite being embarrassed, a part of me felt good that Mrs. Piper had spoken to me, just because at least *someone cared*. Someone was willing to listen to *me* and talk to me and help me—even if I wasn't ready to say much. It felt good because I didn't feel like I could turn to either of my parents. They were both too consumed by their own problems to see me and realize how bad my problems really were.

I went to the Writer's Club room. Since Mrs. Piper had kept me behind, all the others were there when I arrived, but Elliot had saved me a seat beside him.

Mr. Brown led a standard rotational writing exercise with the group. He gave us the first two lines of a story, and we had to go from there. When he said stop, we had to stop, even if it meant stopping in mid-sentence, and we passed our papers to the person on the left. Then we began with the next person's paper. At the end of the workshop, we read all the stories out loud.

Elliot stopped me when we picked up our coats to leave. "You were late."

"Mrs. Piper kept me after study hall to talk about something."

"Everything okay?"

"Yeah." I didn't want to tell him that she thought I was an alcoholic. It was stupid. I was still embarrassed by the whole thing. "I'm an artist, you know. I took her class every year until this one."

"Cool, I didn't know that. What do you like best—oils? Watercolors? Charcoal?"

"Everything. It's hard to choose. I love sculpture. I love drawing. In paint... I think I like acrylic best."

"So why didn't you take it this year?"

"I took physiology instead." I made a face.

"Brilliant tradeoff."

"Actually, I like that class a lot, too. Anatomy is interesting. I like seeing how we fit together. All the different systems are pretty amazing, you know. Nervous, muscular, skeletal—what they can do."

"*Life* is pretty amazing," he said. His blue-green eyes bore into mine for emphasis.

I nodded. Around us, the room had emptied and fallen silent. Even Mr. Brown, who often lingered to talk to someone about a critique, had made a beeline for the parking lot this afternoon.

"What are you doing tonight?" His voice turned silky.

"Writing."

He lowered his face closer to mine. "Bring more pages tomorrow."

My heart went into overdrive at his proximity. I lifted my chin and shook my head. "Only if they're ready."

He studied my face a moment. I wondered what he was thinking. His expression was inscrutable. I hoped mine was, too.

"How did your finals go?" he asked.

Oh, that.

"Good, all A's and B's." My throat closed up. Dang, I wished I was a better actress. I tried smiling.

"Really?"

I nodded.

"I seem to remember you telling me that you needed to score a hundred percent on your Calculus final—and Physics too—to keep your straight A's." His eyes never left mine, and he literally had me backed against the wall, clutching my winter coat like a shield between us.

"Uh-huh."

"So, did you?"

I swallowed. I wished this conversation wasn't happening. I wanted the electricity to go out or something, but Elliot just kept staring at me and waiting for an answer.

"No." I lowered my head. My throat burned at this admission, which I'd now made twice in the same day. I added, "But report cards don't come out until next week. I was close. Maybe with extra credit...or some other points that I forgot to include...maybe I'll still earn the A."

"Maybe you won't. Then what?"

Tears threatened to spill. I dodged around a desk and began putting on my coat, heading for the door.

"Kim!" He chased after me and grabbed my arm.

"No, let me go!"

Instead, he swung me around to face him again and grabbed both my shoulders. He gave me a little shake. "You promised me!"

"And I haven't broken any promises. I told you I'm going home to write. I told you that report cards come out next week, and maybe I'll still get the A. Nothing's happened. Nothing's changed."

We stared at one another.

"Everything's changed," he whispered.

I nodded. He understood! My story must have been halfway decent because he actually understood it. I gave him a sad smile. "Yeah, but today, everything's still the same, too."

I looped my arm through his and walked with him to the parking lot. "See you tomorrow," I said.

We stood at my car, looking at one another. Suddenly, he crushed me against his chest, those strong biceps wrapping around me, and then his hands moved up to the sides of my face, cupping my cheeks and pulling my face to his. His lips pressed hard and warm against mine. It was over in a second.

Outside in the dark, his eyes looked blank and cold as he turned away.

On the way home, I ran my tongue over my tingling lips and replayed the conversation in my mind, wondering if I should have lied to Elliot about my final exams, just so he wouldn't worry. I hated that look on his face when we parted. That look canceled out all the magic I might have felt about our first—and probably last—kiss.

When I opened the front door, Mom was sitting on the couch, watching TV. Cigarette smoke filled the small living room. I hung my coat in the closet and kicked off my boots.

"Hey," I said, flopping down beside her.

"How was school?"

"Boring. How was work?"

"Boring."

I picked up the TV remote and asked, "What are you watching?"

"Commercials. And every now and then, a sitcom rerun comes on for a few minutes."

A pizza commercial played. My stomach roared. Peanut butter crackers didn't fill me up for long. "What's for dinner?" I asked.

"Whatever you'd like to make."

I went into the kitchen and studied the pantry. Then the freezer. Not much to choose from. A bag of frozen peas. A box of frozen waffles. A frozen pot pie. Sausage.

"How about spaghetti?" I called out. A half wall of cabinets separated the living room and kitchen areas, so we couldn't see each other but could hear okay.

"That's fine," she said. "I think there's some sausage in the freezer to put in the sauce."

"I know, I found it."

I began cooking spaghetti. The activity helped me push the conversation with Elliot to the back of my mind for awhile. After dinner I went into my room to work on my story. I had to incorporate the changes that Elliot had suggested, as well as continue with the ending. I felt pressure because time was running out and I wanted this story to be my best work ever. It had to be. It was my last story. Everybody would read it. It had to be perfect.

18. Apothecary

November 6

On Thursday before school, I counted the pills in Mom's prescription bottle again. She'd only taken three since my last count, but I wanted to be sure there were enough. Fourteen. I needed more than that. Thirty seemed like a better number.

I dialed the phone number of the pharmacy on the label. The automated menu gave me an option to refill the prescription, and I entered the code. The program confirmed a refill and gave me a pickup time for this afternoon. Was that okay? I pushed the button to confirm and hung up.

I rubbed my hands up and down my legs. Okay. Okay. I needed to go to school.

In Honor's English class, Mr. Brown handed out literature textbooks. "As much as I'd like to spend the entire year improving your writing and critical thinking skills," he said, "the Board of Education wants us to cover the classics as well."

We read a couple of poems and talked about them, and he gave us a reading assignment for tomorrow.

On my way to Gym, I stopped to say hi to Elliot. Things had been weird between us since Tuesday night. No mention of the kiss or my grades. We tried to act the same as before any of that happened, but even Donna took me aside after lunch on Wednesday and asked what was wrong. I didn't tell her anything.

"Hey," I said to Elliot.

"Hi." His face relaxed into a smile. "How are you this morning?"

"Good. You?"

"You look tired." His smile dropped a little with concern, and his face tilted to the side. "How much did you sleep?"

I frowned. "I don't know. Four or five hours."

He reached out and touched my hand, lightly stroking the back with his finger. "What's wrong?"

My heart speeded up. I didn't know what was going on with us. We acted like a couple, sort of, but weren't. I swallowed and murmured, "Nothing, I was just writing, and time slipped away from me."

"Oh! Did you bring some more pages for me?"

"I don't have anything ready yet," I hedged. "I've put in your comments, but I'm stuck on some plot points. I need to focus some more over the weekend." I stared at the floor because looking at his face was too distracting. I couldn't keep my balance.

"Maybe I could help you brainstorm."

"Yeah, maybe. If I don't come up with anything by Monday, I'll bring what I have and see if you have any ideas."

I raised my chin and smiled, but the truth was that my character was plotting her final days, and I couldn't share any of that with him at this point. He had to wait to see the ending at the same time as everyone else.

He seemed to search my eyes. "Okay, good. See you at lunch?"

"Yeah."

Heart pounding, I hurried to Gym. While the first set of girls played a volleyball game, I sat on the bleachers and wrapped my arms around my stomach. It burned. Things were too complicated. It was black-and-white a month ago: *get straight A's or die.* The dying part was turning out to be harder than I expected. I was lying to people I loved—my best friend, my mom, Elliot, teachers. This story was dragging on and on. I needed to wrap it up fast.

What if Mom found out about the prescription? She'd ask questions I wouldn't be able to answer. I should have waited until closer to report cards before calling in the refill. What if she tried to refill it herself in the next week and discovered that she couldn't? That was stupid.

I needed to pull myself together.

Calculus and Physics passed in a daze. At lunch, Elliot sat with us again, and he joked with my friends. I could tell that everyone liked him. I couldn't stop smiling. I still couldn't believe someone as good looking as him went to my school—and talked to me. I was afraid I'd say the wrong thing, and he'd disappear.

Later that afternoon when I arrived at Writer's Club, the room was still dark. I flipped on the lights and headed toward the back of the room to see if anyone else had turned in new work that needed to be reviewed. Elliot was already standing there.

"Why were you in the dark?" I asked.

"Covert operation." He smiled crookedly. I took in his good looks in one breath and blushed.

"Should I leave?" I asked.

"Too late. Now I have to kill you."

"Oh, okay." I nodded.

He continued smiling at me. "Aren't you curious?" he asked.

"Honestly, I'm afraid to ask."

"Nothing special. I had some late critique worksheets. Did you need something from here? I could move out of your way."

He didn't move out of my way.

"I was just checking to see if any new work had been turned in," I said.

"Amy has a new poem. Did you see it?"

"No." I stepped around him to the filing cabinet and took the folder.

He stood close behind me. "Another sappy love poem, I'm afraid..." He lowered his voice. "And not a very good one."

I took a step backwards, so that I was trapped between the filing cabinet, the wall, and him.

He chuckled. "Why do you look so nervous?"

"Bad poetry sets me on edge."

"You're only taking my word for it that it's bad."

"You have pretty good judgment—about poetry."

"Not people?" he asked.

I shrugged. "I can't answer that."

"Why not?"

"I don't know you well enough. For all I know, you might think Mr. Vernon is the greatest educator of all time or have posters of Nicholas Cage plastered all over your bedroom."

He smirked. "Definitely not."

"Glad to hear it."

Writer's corner had never felt so small...or hot. Breathing became difficult.

"We should do something about this," Elliot murmured. His blue-green eyes bore into mine.

"Should we?" I wasn't sure what he was talking about.

"We should." He took a step toward me. I had nowhere to go.

"Do what?"

He pressed me against the wall and lowered his voice to a husky whisper. "We should go out."

I gulped.

He chuckled. "What are you worried about?"

"So many things."

"You *have* gone on a date before, haven't you?"

"Hmm." I bit my lip. His eyes widened. "I had a boyfriend when I was a freshman," I said. "But my parents didn't allow me to go out on a *date* date—like, alone in a car with a boy date—until I turned sixteen, and by then we'd broken up."

"Why no one else?"

"I've been pretty focused on academics."

"Right...November." He moved even closer to me. "Are your parents still making you crazy?"

I thought about the news Mom had given me about the affair. Everything seemed different now. "Um...they're in a holding pattern. Dad doesn't ask about Mom much anymore, which is good."

"Still no talk of divorce?"

I shook my head. "It's coming. Probably once one of them starts dating."

Other students came through the door to the Writer's Club room. Elliot smiled at me and stepped backwards. "So you never gave me a straight answer. Shall we continue this tomorrow night? Please...say yes."

I nodded, blushing. Mr. Brown walked into the room with a stack of papers. Another wave of students followed him. Elliot and I went to one of the tables and took seats opposite from one another. I snuck a glance at his face while he listened to Mr. Brown.

I had a date with Elliot on Friday night.

As if he knew I was watching, he shifted his eyes to lock with mine. We stared at one another for several seconds. Why hadn't he asked me sooner, when it might have made a difference? Or maybe it wouldn't have made a difference anyway.

"Take out a new sheet of paper," Mr. Brown said.

I dropped my eyes, feeling conflicted.

"Today's exercise is another round-robin," Mr. Brown continued. "We've done that a hundred times. But...is everyone familiar with the story 'The Lottery' by Shirley Jackson?"

He looked around the room.

"Is there anyone who *hasn't* read the story or who doesn't remember the plot?" he asked. "This is important. Our exercise is based on the story."

A few hands went up.

"Okay, good. I like your honesty." Mr. Brown brought his hands together in a single clap. "So quick summary. 'The Lottery' is a story about a town where the lovely townsfolk draw lots to stone someone to death. Only you don't find out that death is the prize for the lottery winner until the end. That's the story's twist."

"I loved that story," Amy said. "Gruesome."

"Indeed," Mr. Brown said. "Your job will be to rewrite Ms. Jackson's masterpiece from the point of view of the lottery winner, in first person. You can let the reader know what's going to happen to the winner, or not. The opening sentence that you're going to start from is: 'I reached into the bucket and drew out my lot.' Five minutes of writing time and then pass to your neighbor. Go!"

I scribbled the first sentence across the top of my page. Already, the story began unfolding in my head. The woman worried about being dead, about what it might be like to be buried in the dirt and the cold, having worms and bugs eating her flesh. She wondered what the moment of death would feel like—the pain. Would her consciousness immediately drift away, or would she remain trapped in the rotting corpse for some period of time and experience the horror of decay in the grave?

What of her spirit? In the end, would she simply blow out, like a candle flame—once here and then gone forever, into oblivion? Or was there something beyond life, a place of love and beauty, the forever home of God?

"Time's up, pass to your...left. Go left," Mr. Brown said.

I took Amy's sheet and scanned what she'd written, and I began writing where she'd left off.

"Come on, Elliot," Mr. Brown said. "Put your pencil down. You're not writing 'Canterbury Tales.'"

I glanced over at Elliot. He lifted his gaze at the same moment, and our eyes met again. I became lost in a sea of aquamarine. His expression was inscrutable. I quickly looked away.

We wrote three more cycles, which meant that Elliot ended up finishing on the paper that I'd started. Mr. Brown asked if someone wanted to read aloud.

"I will!" Elliot said.

"I'm not surprised," Mr. Brown said dryly. "Let's hear what you've written."

He stood and gave a theatrical reading. He managed to make it sound funny and gruesome at the same time. Other students read good pieces, too. Everyone's turned out well. That was the funny thing with this exercise.

"Before everyone leaves," Mr. Brown said, "don't forget that we need to start layout for the upcoming issue of *WordCrafters* in our next meeting. Plan to stay later than usual if you can. There are a few new things in the writer's corner that are ready for critiques, too. Pick up copies on your way out."

I felt a twinge of sadness, realizing that I wouldn't be a part of the production of our next literary publication. Maybe they'd reprint some of my latest story in memory of me or something.

On the way home, I stopped at the pharmacy and walked to the back of the store to pick up the refill. Mr. Thompson handed over the package for me to take to my mom. He'd been refilling my ulcer medicine since junior year, so he knew me and my mom. It was a small town.

I paid the copay, shoved the bottle to the bottom of my backpack, and drove the rest of the way home.

When I opened the door, the trailer smelled delicious. "What are you making?" I asked Mom, kicking off my shoes.

"A casserole," she said. "Some rice, cream of chicken, green beans, and chicken breasts."

"What's the occasion?" I hung my jacket in the closet and went into the living room.

"I needed to do something with that chicken."

"Is it ready?"

"Another half hour or so."

"Guess what?" I said.

"What?"

"I have a date tomorrow night."

She put the TV on mute and turned to look at me, her eyes wide. "Really? Who's the guy?"

"A poet from Writer's Club. A new guy who moved here this year."

"Where are you going?"

"I don't know."

"When are you coming home?"

"Mom."

"Ten o'clock."

"Midnight."

"Eleven."

"Fine."

She un-muted the TV. I sat on the couch beside her, and we chatted until her favorite show came on. She lit another cigarette, and I took my backpack and went to my room. I hid the bottle of pills inside the decorative German beer stein that Dad had given me from when he'd lived in Germany while he was in the Army. It was big, ceramic, and had a hinged metal lid. No one looked in there.

But just in case, I dumped foil-wrapped chocolates over the bottle so that it looked like the beer stein hid my candy stash.

Heart pounding, I flung myself across my bed and opened my journal.

I am going out on a date tomorrow night with Elliot—a.k.a. The Poet. I'm so excited I can hardly believe it. I've really fallen for him. What do I do if he starts kissing me again, if we're alone, and…?

I'm going to die anyway next week. This could be my one and only chance for love. I should take it, right? I ought to experience it.

I looked at the page and chewed on the end of my pen. My imagination went into overdrive. I couldn't believe I was even contemplating something like this. Kim the Valedictorian had no time for boys, and sex never entered the realm of possibilities because it led to unplanned pregnancies and ruined lives—never mind the STDs. Kim the Loser, on the other hand, had already ruined her life. A boyfriend could only make things better, not worse.

19. Acoustic

November 7

The next day, Donna pounced on Elliot as soon as he arrived at the cafeteria.

"A date—it's about time! Where are you taking her?" she asked.

"It's a surprise," he said.

"Oh, I love surprises!" she said. "Whisper in my ear."

"You must not understand the meaning of the word *surprise*," he said. "I'm not telling you." He turned and looked at me. "You put up with this all the time?"

I nodded. "She's wonderful, really."

"If you say so."

"Are you going to tell *me* where we're going?" I asked.

"You'll know when we arrive." He smiled mischievously.

"How should I dress?"

He stepped back and looked at me, one finger over his mouth, thumb under his chin, eyes narrowed. He circled around me. Donna rolled her eyes. "Oh good grief."

"What you have on is fine," he said.

"I'm not wearing the same thing that I wore to school today," I said. "Don't you know anything about girls?"

"Jeans. Casual."

"Okay, I know now." I leaned closer to him. "You're taking me to a club, aren't you? We're going to hear your band."

"I can't get you a fake ID in a day."

"Oh." My face fell.

He laughed and shook his head. "I don't have a fake ID either. I don't drink when I go there, remember?"

"Oh yeah."

"We're *not* going to a club, but that's all I'm going to say. Let's talk about something else."

"Jason took Donna to see that new zombie movie," I said. "She said it was pretty good."

"I heard they didn't follow the book at all."

"There was a book?" Donna asked.

Her face screwed up into such a comical expression of surprise that Elliot and I looked at each other and busted out laughing.

"Yes," Elliot said. "There is a *literary masterpiece*." He spent the next ten minutes going over the entire plot. I couldn't believe he remembered it in such detail.

Afternoon classes passed slowly. I wanted the day to be over. In study hall, I joined Lonnie and the others in playing cards again instead of doing homework, even though Mrs. Piper gave me a sour look. I didn't care. Well, not much anyway.

On the drive home, I ran a mental inventory of my closet, trying to decide what to wear on the date. Mom wasn't there when I arrived. I jumped in the shower.

Half an hour later, I was blow-dried and made up again, with a clean pair of jeans and a cute sweater. I flopped onto the couch and nervously surfed through channels.

Mom came home from work, and I helped her unload groceries from the trunk. While we were putting things away, headlights flashed across the front windows, and a car pulled into the driveway. He was here.

I threw the last of the cold items into the refrigerator before he knocked on the door. I crossed the floor in a few steps and answered it. Elliot came inside. He hooked his thumbs in the front pockets of his jeans and gave me a crooked smile, black hair slightly tousled from the wind.

"Mom, this is Elliot," I said. "Elliot, my mom."

"Very nice to meet you," Elliot said to her.

"Same here."

"Okay, let's go," I said. We didn't need a game of twenty questions.

"Where are you kids going?" Mom asked.

Elliot cut his eyes at me and smiled.

"I have no idea, Mom," I said. "He says it's a surprise."

"I can understand that you might be uncomfortable with that," Elliot said. He walked over to my mom and cupped his hand beside her ear, whispering something. Her eyes widened slightly, and then she nodded.

"And what time do you plan to have her home?" she asked.

"How late can I have her out?" he asked.

I think he mesmerized Mom with those aquamarine eyes, too. "Midnight," she said.

I wasn't going to remind her that she'd told *me* I had to be home at eleven.

"She will be inside the house at midnight," he assured her.

Mom smiled. "All right then, you kids have fun."

I took a step toward the door and pushed on his shoulder. "Go, quick."

We hurried out to the car. As soon as we buckled in and he started the engine, I said, "Okay, the suspense has been killing me. Where are we going?"

"It's going to keep killing you because you have to wait."

"You're going to tell my mother, but not me?"

"That's right."

While he drove, I looked around the inside of his car. "You keep it really nice in here. Not a stray French fry in sight."

He laughed. "I usually run the vacuum whenever I spray it off at the car wash."

"Are you a neat freak?"

"I like to take care of my things. Call it what you like."

My stomach growled—very loudly.

Blushing, I said, "I hope that wherever we're going involves food."

"Oh, sure. Here." He reached into his pocket. I heard the crackling of a wrapper, and a second later, he handed me a package of peanut butter crackers.

"Thanks…" I rolled my eyes.

"Kidding. You will eat a real meal tonight, not crackers. Not macaroni and cheese."

"Macaroni and cheese is one of the food groups—dairy."

He smirked and shook his head. After a short drive into town, he parked in front of a small Italian restaurant on Main Street and turned off the car. "You like it here?"

"I do."

The place was busy, but the hostess put us into an empty booth along the wall near the back. The tables were covered with red and white checkered tablecloths. Our napkins had the same pattern.

I shrugged out of my coat. When I looked up, Elliot was staring at me. He wore a black shirt, and his vibrant eyes seemed to glow. "What?" I asked.

"So this is your first date."

Shaking my head, I mumbled, "I *never* should have told you that."

"You're right," he said. "Now I feel all this pressure to make it perfect."

I smiled. "No pressure from me. Let's just enjoy ourselves."

"So you won't hate me if I spill my drink or something?"

"No."

"That's a relief." He mock-swiped at his forehead.

"Since when did you become so insecure? You're usually Mr. Confident."

"Perhaps…" He leaned forward, his hand not quite touching mine. "I am only setting *you* at ease, so that *you* will stop worrying about the pressure to make everything perfect."

I frowned. "I'm not worried."

"Good."

"I *wasn't* worried...until now."

A server came to our table. "Can I bring you anything to drink?" she asked.

Elliot nodded at me to go first.

"Just water," I said.

"Coke," he said.

"Okay, I'll be right back to take your orders."

As soon as she left, I picked up the menu. "Guess I'd better look at this," I said. "Do you already know what you want?"

"Yes."

"What are you ordering?"

"I'm not telling." He cocked his eyebrow at me. "Pick your own."

I tried to hide my smile—and failed. "Fine."

I studied the options for a few minutes. When the waitress returned with our drinks, she asked, "Are you ready?"

"I'll have a calzone," I said. "Sausage, pepperoni, and green peppers."

"And you, sir?" she asked Elliot.

"The same. That sounds good."

I opened my mouth in protest, then snapped my jaw shut. Elliot grinned. He looked very proud of himself.

"Excellent," our server said. "I'll have these out to you shortly."

I glared at him. He just kept smiling.

When our server left, he leaned forward, elbows on the table, and asked, "How's the story coming?"

I shrugged. "Okay."

"Broken through your block?"

"Not exactly, but I think I'll have everything resolved by the end of the weekend. I'm going to work on it tomorrow."

"So I'll see pages on Monday?"

"I expect to have a complete draft done. Maybe even ready for Tuesday's Writer's Club."

"I can hardly wait."

I swallowed hard and looked at the table. Tuesday was the day that report cards came out. The story would definitely be done.

"How about you?" I asked, changing the subject. "Any new poems?"

"A song. That's the surprise. I'm taking you somewhere tonight where I can play and sing it for you."

"Really?" Excitement raised the pitch of my voice. "Now I just want dinner to hurry up and be over so we can go to the good part."

He stretched his hand across the table and clasped mine. "Dinner will be a good part, too. Calzone is better than peanut butter crackers."

"Are you sure? Have you ever actually eaten a peanut butter cracker?" I teased.

"On occasion, yes. And calzones are better."

"What's the title of your song?"

He chuckled and stroked the back of my hand with his thumb. Electric tingles shot up my arm. "You *really* don't like surprises at all, do you?"

"No, not really."

"Mmm." We stared at one another for a few minutes, and then he said, "Your mom seemed really nice."

"You want to talk about *my mom?*"

"A subject change seemed necessary."

"Sure, my mom's nice." I raised my eyebrows. Okay mister, where do you want to go from there?

"She's a nurse?" he asked.

"The scrubs? No, nurse's aide. She works in a nursing home."

"You don't look like her."

"I look like my dad, even more like my grandmother on his side. What about you? Where do those amazing eyes come from?"

He smiled. "Amazing, huh?"

I scowled. "Mom or Dad?"

"Mom." That goofy grin never left his face.

"Stop smiling. I'll never give you another compliment."

"It was just so surprising," he said.

Please! Guys like him always knew how gorgeous they were—right? He had to know the effect he had on girls. I looked around the restaurant, wondering if anyone we knew was here. Nope. Slowly, I brought my gaze back around to Elliot.

"Still here," he said, squeezing my hand for emphasis.

He could be very good at posing. Looking good. "If you want to be an actor, why aren't you in the drama club?" I asked.

He blinked. "Major subject change."

"Not really. Answer, please?"

"Mr. Reynolds and I don't see eye-to-eye. Writer's Club conflicted. Pick your reasons."

"Did you mean it that you want to go to New York and act on Broadway?" I asked.

"I want to go to New York. I might try acting. I could try song writing. Who knows?"

"You don't have a *plan*?" I didn't understand how anyone could bungle through life without knowing where they were heading. Move to New York and *just see*? Crazy!

"Even the best plans fall apart," he said.

"So your philosophy is to not bother making a plan at all?"

"Life has a way of working out."

"Sometimes it doesn't." I thought about my grades in Calculus and Physics.

"Even when it *seems* like things aren't working out, they are. They're just not working out the way you wanted or hoped. Things are going in a different direction."

"How did you become such an optimist?"

"How did *you* become such a *pessimist*?" He raised his eyebrows.

"Heartbreak."

"How does a girl who's never been on a date get her heart broken?"

"I'm not talking about romantic heartbreak," I said. "I remember once, when I was ten or eleven, my parents bought a used car. We never had new cars, but this was a pretty good car, and it was new to us. Good condition. We were driving home from somewhere, and another car hit us—totaled the car and put both of my parents in the hospital. Mom couldn't work for awhile. I remember that they only had liability insurance on the car. They kept saying that, and it meant that they couldn't replace it. Our house was full of heartbreak for a long time after that accident."

"That sounds awful."

"I'm not telling you that to feel sorry for myself. It's just a fact. That's why I'm not an optimist. Things don't always work out."

"But they did. You're here. Your parents are alive, working, driving."

"I really don't want you to show me the positive in that situation."

"Sorry."

Our server picked that moment to come around the corner with our plates. "Can I bring you anything else?" she asked.

"I don't think so," Elliot said. "You?"

I shook my head.

"This looks good." He picked up his fork and wiggled his eyebrows. "Good choice."

I rolled my eyes and unwrapped my silverware from the napkin. We fell silent while we ate. I couldn't help wondering where he would take me to hear his songs. His home? Would I meet his parents? I wanted to listen to his music, but an introduction with the folks was really unexpected. I'd pictured dinner and maybe a movie.

After we finished eating, he asked, "What are you thinking about?"

"Your surprise."

He smiled. "Does that mean you're ready to leave?"

I nodded and looked at my plate. "It was a lot of food."

"Especially for you."

"Better than peanut butter crackers. You were right."

"Glad you liked it."

When the server came around again, he gave her money for the bill, and we put on our coats and left the restaurant. Elliot opened the car door for me. I buckled up and rubbed my hands together to warm them while he came around the front.

"I think the temperature fell ten degrees while we were eating," he said.

"Welcome to the east coast. Do you miss California now?"

"Nope."

"Did something happen to make you hate it so much?"

He gave me a sideways glance. "Heartbreak. The romantic kind."

"Oh."

He chuckled. "It feels like a very long time ago, now."

He started the car and pulled away from the curb. I stared out the windshield and wondered what his ex-girlfriend in California would have been like. I imagined movie-star beauty and wealth, and the personality of a Pomeranian.

"So are we going to your house?" I asked.

"Nope."

"No? Then where?"

"You must have been really difficult to surprise at Christmas when you were a kid."

"My parents had to keep the presents at a friend's house," I admitted. "Otherwise, I searched until I found them."

"We'll be there in about five minutes. Just relax."

I sighed in frustration.

He drove down the main highway for awhile and then turned onto a secondary road that I didn't know. The road twisted up a wooded hill. Snow had started falling in earnest while we were in the restaurant, and the flakes seemed to sparkle like diamonds as the headlights hit them. Music played at a low volume from the car stereo. I kept quiet, waiting.

The car climbed one hill, then another, and then turned into the driveway of a large A-frame house with trees scattered through the front yard. A few lights burned inside, but there weren't any other cars in the driveway.

Elliot put the car into park and shut off the engine. "We're here."

"Your house?"

"One of the guys in the band lives here…with his parents. But tonight, we have the place to ourselves until 2 a.m. Come on."

His expression changed. He looked uncertain now— and a little anxious.

I followed him inside, feeling a little nervous too. He took me to the basement, where there was an upright piano along the wall, guitar stands, and drums set up for practice. "Do you come here to listen to them practice?" I asked.

"For the new songs, yeah."

I touched the piano. "You play?"

"Ten years of lessons." He shoved his hands in the front pockets of his jeans.

"Let's hear it." I smiled.

"I suddenly have stage fright." His voice sounded lighthearted, but his expression was serious.

"Should I sit on the couch and cover my eyes so you can pretend that you don't have an audience?"

He cleared his throat. "No, but the song I have for you is better done with this." He picked up an acoustic guitar, took my hand, and led me over to the couch.

He strummed the guitar a few times. Then he began to play a melody. I watched him, transfixed. He sang a verse, and his voice was familiar from some of the things he'd sung in Writer's Club, but different, too. This voice was his serious voice, not a mockery, and it was beautiful. I closed my eyes and listened.

When he finished, I said, "Wow, that was...incredible."

"You liked it?"

"I loved it."

He leaned forward and pressed his lips softly against mine. "I'm glad," he whispered.

My breath caught, and I couldn't take my eyes away from his. Couldn't move. I felt paralyzed by an unfamiliar desire. He smiled and pulled back. I watched him take off the guitar and put it on the floor beside the couch. My lip throbbed where he'd touched it.

He turned back to me with an expression that made muscles deep inside my stomach flutter. I wanted him to kiss me again. His eyes met mine, piercing, and then he leaned forward. This time, his kiss started slow, firm, but grew more demanding. Both his hands moved into my hair, pulling me closer, and his tongue and lips began coaxing mine. His thick arms wrapped around me, and we fell back into the couch, with me lying on top of him, kissing. One of his hands left my hair to explore my shoulders, lower back, and the seat of my jeans. Heat flared everywhere that his fingers traveled.

I raised my own hands to that silky black hair of his that I'd wanted to touch since the day I'd met him, and I pulled his face even closer to mine. It felt so soft. I couldn't believe the feelings racing through my body. Who knew it could feel like this? I'd kissed boys before, but it never made me want to go any further.

He wrapped his arm around my middle, shifted, and suddenly we were lying face to face on our sides on the couch, with me on the inside, cocooned in the warm space. The kissing never stopped. His fingers traveled along my hip and slipped under my sweater. Light as feathers, they shimmied across ribs, traveling north.

I never broke eye contact. I felt captivated by his gaze, which seemed darker than when we were at school together, almost as if he struggled within himself. His breath was harsh.

His fingers reached the underwire of my bra and stopped. They paced back and forth beneath it. For the first time, he closed his eyes and broke the kiss. He sighed.

"What's wrong?" I whispered.

"We should stop."

My heart pounded. "Why?"

He opened his eyes again. "You are so beautiful, Kim. Do you have any idea what I want to do with you right now?"

"I have a pretty good idea."

He tilted his head to the side and smiled. "Really. And you're *okay* with that—on the first date and everything?"

I took a deep breath. It would be easier to just go with it, rather than make an explicit decision that was discussed and agreed upon. When he put it like that, I sounded like a slut or something.

"That's what I thought," he said, pulling away and sitting up.

I sat up too. Why should I care what it sounded like? Report cards came out on Tuesday. Tonight was my one and only chance to experience this. I liked Elliot—a lot. What was so wrong about being with him?

"No, it's okay." I touched his arm. "I want to."

He looked at me, raising his eyebrows. His eyes still burned, but he'd already brought his breathing under control. How did he do that so fast? I still felt like I was on fire.

He cocked his head to the side, as if an idea had just occurred to him.

"Here's a thought," he said. "Let's go out again *next weekend* and celebrate the debut of your story, report cards coming out in November, and your continued good academic standing. We can try this again because you'll still be alive, right?"

I stared at him.

"What's wrong?" he asked.

"If you don't want me, just say so. Don't give me a bunch of excuses and try to humiliate me."

He took my hand. "You misunderstand. I want to. But I like you a lot, and I'm still worried about you. I'm afraid that this…" He waved in the air between us. "This thing that's going on right now is just something on your bucket list."

I shook my head. "*You're* the one who brought me to your friend's empty house. I had no idea what to expect tonight. This is all *your* plan, not mine."

"Right...the music."

"You did sing one song," I conceded.

"Um, yeah." He looked around the room, then down at his lap. He hesitated.

"What?"

He raised his eyes and stared at me with full intensity. "I need to know what you're going to do next week."

My throat began burning and closing up. I thought of the prescription of sleeping pills I'd refilled and stashed in my room. I thought about the goodbye letters I planned on writing this weekend, about the story I'd finish, about all my journals and whether or not I'd burn them. I couldn't say those things to him. All of these actions seemed inevitable now. I didn't see a way to stop.

"I don't know," I whispered.

He closed his eyes, took a deep breath. "Do you remember what you promised me?"

"Yes."

"You'll call me, no matter what." He opened his eyes again.

"Uh-huh."

He stared at me with those gorgeous blue-green eyes for a long time, until I felt like squirming under their scrutiny. At last he released my hand, stood, and went over to a stereo. He fiddled around with his back to me. Music began playing from speakers around the room. He turned off all the lights except some colored ones on a far counter.

He walked back over to the couch and held out his hand. "Dance with me?"

I nodded and stood. The song playing was a ballad but not something I recognized. "Is this one of yours, too?"

"Yes." He folded me into his arms. "I put in a recording that the guys did. It's not professional or anything, but you can hear a good sampling of my songs this way."

I pressed my face against his chest and closed my eyes. We swayed to the music. His strong arms encircled my body and made me feel safe, warm. Here, everything was perfect. Here, my grade point average didn't matter. In this place, in this moment, I could see a life for myself beyond Tuesday.

If only I never had to leave this basement.

20. Admission

November 8

Saturday was cold and gray. Mom was called in to work because someone else was sick, so I had the morning to myself. I called Donna and told her about the date.

"It sounds romantic," she said.

"It was amazing."

"So…we both ended up the guys we wanted. Life is perfect."

I rolled my eyes. "There's more to life than guys."

"What could be more important than true love?"

"Jason is your true love?" I asked, surprised.

"Duh!"

"How do you know?"

"How do I know what?"

"That it's True Love—not just a crush or something."

"I just *know*," she said. "It's about how he makes me feel, the way I can't stop thinking about him, the whole package. Why? You don't think you love Elliot?"

"I don't know," I admitted. "Love is such a scary admission—so binding. Can't I just be in Serious Like with him?"

She laughed. "You can be whatever you are."

"I want to go out with him again."

"I think you're falling for him, whether you admit it or not."

"You're probably right," I agreed. I glanced at the clock. "What are you doing today?"

"Getting my hair done and going to the tanning bed. Later this afternoon, we're going over to Grandma and Grandpa's house for a big family celebration. It's Aunt Vivian's eightieth birthday."

"Sounds fun."

"What about you?"

"Just hanging out here…writing, homework, maybe watch a movie."

"I think I'm going to have more fun than you."

After we hung up, I went into the kitchen and fixed some hot tea to fight the chill of the day. Then I worked on my story for several hours and finished the draft. Finally! It needed some edits, but at last I had a complete manuscript from beginning to end.

On the last page, Mandy, the main character, committed suicide.

The End. For her—and for me.

I just needed to finish writing my goodbye letters, and then I would be ready.

21. Adieu

November 10

On Monday, the day before report cards came out, I went to Dad's house after school to say goodbye. Driving down my childhood road, tears began to blur my vision. Everything had gone so wrong. When I'd lived here, I'd been number one, and my dreams for the future looked bright and achievable. Now I had no future at all.

Dad was already home when I pulled into the driveway. I swiped away the moisture beneath my eyes and fixed my mascara before going inside.

"If I'd known you were coming, I would've stopped at the store and picked up something for dinner," he said.

I shrugged and dropped my bag on the counter. "That's okay."

"I think I have a box of macaroni and cheese in the cupboard."

"I'm not hungry right now, Dad."

"I am." He patted his belly. "I was just fixing a snack when you drove up."

"Go ahead, knock yourself out."

I sat at the kitchen table and watched him drag the lunchmeat, cheese, and mayonnaise from the refrigerator. I thought again about what Mom told me about her reason for leaving him.

"Are all those women still chasing you at work?" I asked.

"Since the ladies found out that I'm single, they've started bringing me coffee. I go to the bathroom, and when I return, there are three or four fresh cups sitting on my desk!"

"Why?"

Pointing to his checkered flannel shirt, he said, "Apparently, I'm a hot item."

I smiled and rolled my eyes. "Again, *why?*"

He winked at me. "You may see a bald, overweight, 40-year-old man, but your dad's a real charmer."

"So I hear." I couldn't keep the edge from my voice.

His smile dropped. We stared at each other. Suddenly I wanted him to admit what he'd done.

"Kim…"

"What? Just say it."

"I don't know what your mother told you—"

"Why don't *you* tell me?" My eyes burned.

"It's between me and your mother. I don't think it's any of your business."

"Why not? I lost my home, too. I lost my family, too. I lost everything! Don't I have a right to know?" My voice became shrill. Tears were leaking out of my eyes. I hadn't intended to bring this up. I'd just wanted a nice evening with my dad before report cards came out.

"I'm sorry," he said. "It happened. It was a mistake. I'm sorry."

"Are you still seeing her?"

"No." He shook his head.

"How long were you together?"

He sighed. "Kim, I'm sorry I hurt you. I'm sorry I hurt your mother. I wish I could take it back."

"You can't."

"I know that."

"You ruined *everything*," I whispered. In that moment I wanted to tell him that I'd gotten B's in Physics and Calculus because of him, because he'd destroyed our home, and now I was going to commit suicide, and all of it was his fault. I felt so angry and sad, all at the same time.

"I know, I screwed up big time," he said.

I swiped the tears on my cheeks.

"Are we okay?" he asked. "That's all that matters to me. I can lose everything as long as I know that you and I are still okay. Then I can make it."

My eyes slid to the ground. I nodded.

"I love you, sweetheart." While I wasn't looking, he grabbed me into a hug.

"Ugh, Dad. I love you too."

He released me. "Okay?"

"Okay." I nodded.

"So I could eat?"

I rolled my eyes. "Don't let me stop you."

He finished assembling his Dagwood-sized "snack" sandwich and changed the subject. "How's school?" he asked.

At the mention of my grades I felt my eyes burning again. I shrugged and choked out, "Okay."

He carried the packages and condiments back to the refrigerator. "Just okay?"

Helplessly, I swiped at the tears as they began streaming down my cheeks again. What was wrong with me? He was going to start asking all sorts of questions.

"What's wrong?" Dad stared at me.

"You don't want to know," I said, trying to do damage control with humor. "PMS, a boy, my stomach's bothering me again...It's a perfect storm."

"Who's this boy?"

Leave it to Dad to focus on that part of the sentence. "A poet in Writer's Club."

"How serious is he?"

"Don't worry, we only went on one date." I sniffed and wiped the moisture on my face.

"Where did you go?"

"That Italian restaurant in town, on Main Street."

He narrowed his eyes. "Let's move into the living room. I want to hear more about him."

"There's nothing to say." I followed him. "And anyway, I'm over sixteen now. I'm allowed to date. Your rules, remember?"

"Did I say sixteen? I meant twenty-one."

"Dad!"

He collapsed onto the couch with his sandwich. "Who's this guy's father?"

"You don't know his family. They just moved here over the summer."

"Where do they live?"

"I don't know. We didn't go to his house. Will you *stop*, Dad? It was just a date. And we probably won't go out again."

He took a bite of his sandwich and regarded me silently for several seconds while he chewed. "You said your stomach's bothering you again, too?" he asked.

Thank goodness he changed the subject. "Yeah. I just keep drinking antacid and taking my medicine. That helps a little."

He shook his head. "You're too young to have an ulcer."

"We've had that conversation before, Dad. It's not like I have a choice in the matter."

"You put too much pressure on yourself."

I raised my eyebrows and looked sideways at him. Yes I put pressure on myself, but didn't he realize that he put equal pressure on me?

"You took your finals last week, didn't you?" he asked.

"Yep."

"How'd you do?"

"Pretty good."

"Still the valedictorian?"

I couldn't let him down—not on this last night with him. "You bet," I said.

"That's my girl!"

"I've never studied so hard in my life," I said truthfully.

He grunted and took another bite of his sandwich. I watched him eat for a few minutes. I thought about all the things we could possibly talk about today. I certainly didn't want to dwell on my grades.

"What do you think happens to us when we die?" I asked when he finished chewing.

He licked mayonnaise off he fingers and regarded me. "Worms eat us."

I threw a pillow at him. "That's it? You don't think there's any afterlife?"

He narrowed his eyes. "Where's this question coming from?"

Lies rolled easily from my tongue tonight. I'd become the author, the expert storyteller. "We had a boy commit suicide in our school a month ago, remember? Kids keep talking about it. Some are still seeing the school counselor."

"Oh, yeah, I remember that."

"So, what happens?"

"I don't know."

"Dad!"

"What?" He put his empty plate on the coffee table and sat straighter.

"You're the adult. You're supposed to know, or say something wise and comforting and...*parental*."

"Death is life's greatest mystery," he said. "Everyone wonders, and everyone finds out."

"Very profound."

"Thank you, I tried."

"What do *you* believe?" I asked.

"I believe in God." He shrugged and looked at me. "I believe in an afterlife. What do *you* believe?"

"I think it's like going to sleep, like shutting off the light and never waking up. You just stop existing."

"No afterlife?" He looked concerned. I didn't realize Dad had such religious leanings. I'd never seen him step foot in a church.

"After*sleep*," I corrected. "Rest for the weary." To me, this sounded like heaven. I did not want an afterlife where they forced me to play in the harp band for eternity.

"You're okay believing that your school friend just doesn't exist anymore, anywhere?" he asked.

School friend? Oh, right, he thought we were talking about Tim Maiers.

How did I feel about *me* not existing anymore?

"Tim still exists through the things he did," I said carefully. "He exists through the things he made and left behind." I had no idea if Tim created anything, but in thinking of myself, that's how I would continue to exist. I would leave my words behind. "He also exists in the hearts of his friends and the people who loved him."

He stared at me for a moment. I suddenly felt like he had super powers and could read my mind. He knew I was lying about my grades and that I was telling him goodbye. Tears rose in my eyes again. I sniffled.

"I'm sorry about your friend," he said. "I know how hard it can be to lose someone like that."

"You do?"

He nodded. "I had a friend commit suicide around the holidays one year. His wife had left him. He'd lost his job. He lost hope. It was a terrible thing."

He puckered his lips and stared down at his lap for a minute.

"There's always hope, Kim. Don't ever forget that. Even when things seem their very darkest, there's always hope. But once you're dead, you're dead forever."

I glanced at the shotgun leaning against the wall. I thought about my fears of him sitting here alone at night, oiling the metal, feeling depressed and angry about the separation with Mom.

"Did *you* ever feel like suicide?" I asked.

"No."

I didn't quite believe him. "Really?"

"We only get this one life. Just one."

I looked at my hands. "But it's a mystery, right? Maybe there's reincarnation, many lives."

"I only know for sure about this one."

We didn't talk much anymore. After awhile, I fixed a sandwich for my own dinner, and we watched the evening news together. It was nice, just hanging out with my dad.

When I got home that evening, Mom stood and turned off the TV. "How was your visit?" she asked.

"Good. Uneventful."

"Did you eat?"

"We had sandwiches," I said.

She nodded and put out her cigarette. "Well, I'm glad you made it home. I was just waiting up for you. I'm going to put my feet up for the night."

"Oh, okay. Goodnight, Mom."

Disappointed, I watched her walk down the hallway and close her bedroom door. So much for spending any of my last evening with her. I guessed I'd better catch her in the morning if I wanted to say goodbye.

I turned out the remaining lights and went to my room. The cat followed me. We sat on my bed, and I wrote in my journal. I'd already written my goodbye letters, and now the story was done, too. I still hadn't decided if I should burn my journals tomorrow or leave them behind. They were so *personal*. I wasn't sure if I wanted anyone to see the real feelings inside me, even after I was gone.

22. Assassination

November 11

When my alarm went off on Tuesday morning, I smelled fresh coffee. It was a half hour earlier than my usual time because I'd wanted to see Mom before she left for work. I shuffled into the kitchen, blinking at the bright light, yawning, and poured some iced tea for myself. Mom sat at the table, already showered, wearing maroon-colored scrubs. She was writing in a notebook.

"You're up early," she said.

"I need to study a little more for a test before heading to school." I was becoming such an expert liar.

"I didn't think a night owl like you could function at this hour."

"I don't *like it*, but it's *possible*, with caffeine." I held up the tea.

"I'm up early doing homework, too." She laughed. "My appointment with Russ is this afternoon."

Russ was her therapist. "He gives you *homework*?"

"Sometimes."

I pulled out a chair and sat beside her. "Like what?"

"A lot of it's private," she said. "It's journaling about certain topics we've discussed, or making lists of things."

I couldn't resist saying, "You've had all week to do your assignment. Why are you waiting until the morning of the day when it's due?"

"I haven't had time."

I smiled. She didn't realize that I was messing with her. She picked up her cigarettes.

"That bad, huh?" I asked.

"You have no idea. All this stuff is coming up, and I'm just feeling so overwhelmed."

I stared at Mom. I loved her, but she had no clue either.

I thought about asking what kind of stuff had come up for her. Why was she so overwhelmed? Listening to her problems was what I did in our relationship. But I wanted something different from her this morning. I wanted her to notice *me* and ask about *me*. Even Dad's twenty questions last night was more welcome than this. At least he cared enough to ask.

Ugh! I didn't want to be mad at her like this. "I need to take a shower and start studying," I said. "Have a good day, Mom."

"You too. See you later tonight."

Except she wouldn't. Tears stung my eyes as I closed the bathroom door and stripped. As I got ready for school, I ran through my plans in my head. Report cards would come out during first period. I would pick up my grades from Mr. Brown, drop off my story in writer's corner after leaving Honor's English, skip school before second period, come home, and take the pills while Mom was still at work. My only logistical question was about when to call Elliot, since I'd promised that I would. I shouldn't call him until the last minute, when I was safely home and beyond rescue.

It seemed like a good plan.

My ulcer burned already. I ate some peanut butter toast before heading out so I wouldn't throw up. I needed my stomach to be able to do a lot of heavy work today.

When I arrived at school, I tried to find Donna to say hi before first bell, but I found out that she was home sick. I would never see my best friend again. All I could think about was our inside jokes and the way she made me laugh. I felt such despair. I'd wanted to say goodbye to her today. I'd written her a letter, but I'd wanted to see her in person, too, one last time, and tease her about Jason.

I couldn't remember what color fingernail polish she'd been wearing yesterday: coral or pink? Maybe a magenta pearl. I would never again see her Floridian bronze tan or the fresh highlights in her hair.

In first period Honor's English class, Mr. Brown passed out report cards without any emotion on his face. They were computer printouts with perforated edges. He didn't even glance at mine. My damning grades were listed in a column down the right side of the page:

HONORS 12 ENG	A
PE (G) 11-12	A
CALCULUS	B
ACC PHYSICS	B
PHYSIOLOGY	A
ACC ECONOMICS	A

All of the lights seemed to go dim, and a huge weight pressed against my chest, making it hard to breathe. Voices sounded far away. A funny taste even coated my tongue. It was really true.

Heidi Jones—the girl who would probably become valedictorian instead of me—sat two rows away. She was no longer number two, but number one. Did she already know that victory was hers? She'd earned straight A's, even in Physics and Calculus, where she'd set the curve for the rest of the class.

She laughed at something someone said and flung her curly hair over her shoulder. Her boyfriend's class ring winked from the chain around her neck.

During class time, Mr. Brown called on someone to read a poem by Dylan Thomas. We talked about Thomas's work and poetic structures in general for a half hour. I couldn't concentrate. My stomach hurt. I felt nervous anticipation as the time passed. I had to get home.

The bell rang. I stood and grabbed my bag. I'd planned to avoid Elliot because seeing him would be too hard, but after learning that Donna was out sick, I suddenly wanted to say goodbye to his face, not just in a phone call.

I left Mr. Brown's classroom and turned left toward our Writer's Club room. Quickly, I ducked in and went to the filing cabinet in the back corner. I put my complete story in the new critique folder.

I glanced around the room. No one saw me.

Still, I hesitated a minute more. This seemed like a bad idea. What if Mr. Brown came in here and read my story during his second period study hall? It would set off alarm bells in his head, and he might call the police before the pills worked. What if Elliot came by and read it too soon?

At the same time, I wanted to be sure that someone *did* read the story at the right time because it was my best work ever, and it explained everything about why I had to do this. Tim Maiers didn't explain himself or his pain. I did. On these pages. But I couldn't depend on my mom to read them—even if I left my story on the table with my letters. My parents never read my stories. I needed someone *here* to read it, someone dependable who would understand.

I took a deep breath, turned, and stepped into the hall again. I headed toward the gym and Elliot. I looked over my shoulder once to see if anyone went into the Writer's Club room, but no one did. I felt very nervous having that story out of my hands. I had to get home quickly now.

I passed the door of the janitor's closet. Ahead, Elliot was leaning against the wall outside his classroom. He looked hot, as always, and those blue-green eyes found me across the ocean of students that separated us. He smiled. I walked over to him and leaned against the wall, too.

"Do you have any plans tonight?" he asked.

I looked at him, frowning. Where was this coming from? "Writer's club," I said.

"After that."

"Why?"

"I've finally convinced my mom to let me have a dog," he said. "I want you to come to the Humane Society with me and help me pick one out."

"You're getting a *dog?*"

"Yep." He nodded, beaming.

"What are you going to do with it when you go to college?" I asked.

"I'm not sure I want to go to college. Like I said, I think I'm going to move to New York and just live for a year or so first, and figure out what I want to do."

"Dogs cost a lot," I pointed out. "It will be harder and more expensive to rent an apartment if you have one."

"Whose side are you on?"

"I'm just saying that it's a big decision and commitment."

"Noted."

He stared at me with pouting lips. I couldn't help remembering the feel of those lips pressed against mine or wishing for one more night like that one. Didn't he say that we could go out again this coming Friday and make out—if I was still alive?

I was too far gone to be saved by kisses.

"So?" he asked.

"I'm sorry…what?"

"Will you go with me?"

"Oh, to the Humane Society tonight. I didn't talk you out of it?"

"No," he said. The corners of his lips curved upwards.

"Let me think about it. I have to go to class."

"What's to think about?"

I pushed away from the wall. "Goodbye, Elliot."

He narrowed his eyes. Those gorgeous eyes that I fell in love with. For a moment, I became distracted by those long black eyelashes. I really wanted to kiss him, but that would raise too many red flags. I took a deep breath, turned, and walked away.

I continued toward the gym until I passed out of his line of sight, and then I turned down another hall that would take me to the parking lot and my car. I'd parked on the side of the school, and exiting the building through that door unnoticed was pretty easy because people were coming and going all the time for Driver's Education and some of the other classes over there.

On the way home I drove recklessly, pushing the accelerator to the floor, but I still made it to the trailer alive. It took about twenty-five minutes. I parked and pulled my phone out of my bag. Three missed calls from Elliot. Uh-oh. He suspected something. I never should have told him goodbye.

I stuffed the phone into my pocket. My ulcer felt like it was on fire. I went inside and threw my school stuff into the corner. There wasn't much time. It wouldn't be that many hours before Mom came home from work, and I needed to be "asleep" before then.

I did not want to wake up in the hospital with some doctors pumping my stomach. I'd heard that experience was pretty horrible.

I picked up one of the sharp paring knives that lay in the sink and touched the blade to my wrist. I supposed if I really wanted to be sure, I could do this. No chances.

But I was a big baby. I hated blood. That's why I hadn't taken one of Dad's guns. I just wanted to go to sleep and never wake up. I just wanted to stop hurting.

I went to the bathroom and opened the medicine cabinet. I grabbed the open bottle of sleeping pills and a glass of water and went to my room. The cat jumped onto the bed. I reached into the beer stein and pulled out the additional bottle that I'd refilled at the pharmacy. I opened my desk. The goodbye letters I'd written were kept here. I leaned them neatly against my lamp. Then I turned on my radio so I could listen to some music. I unscrewed the prescription bottle.

My phone rang.

I sat on my bed with a handful of sleeping pills.

My phone rang again. It was probably Elliot.

I put the pills back into the bottle, recapped it, and looked at the caller ID. Unknown number. I picked up anyway.

"Hello?"

"Kim?" A male voice.

"Yes." I frowned.

"This is Mr. Brown."

Mr. Brown? I was very confused. "Yes?"

"I just finished reading your story."

Oh, no.

"How?" I asked. "It's long, and I just turned it in after first period."

I looked at my watch. The story had been in the folder just under an hour. He must have picked it up right after I dropped it off—and went through it like a speed-reader.

"That's why I called. You've written a real page-turner. This is your best work ever."

I narrowed my eyes. "Why did you call me? You could have just said this at Writer's Club. How did you get this number, anyway?"

"Like your other stories lately, the ending of this one is disturbing," he said. "So I went looking for you in class, but no one knew where you were. You'd skipped Gym. Where are you, Kim?"

"This is a truancy call?"

"It *started* as the Writer's Club advisor wanting to give feedback on a great story," he said. "Now, it's a concerned teacher wondering about a missing student. You're no longer on school grounds, are you?"

I looked around my bedroom. "No..."

"Are you at home?"

"No," I lied. The last thing I wanted was for him to send the police here.

"Are you going to tell me where you are?"

"The mall."

"I doubt that." He sighed. "Do you have any study halls this afternoon?"

"Seventh period."

"Any chance you could wrap up your shopping and come back to school to meet with me? I have some markups I want to go over with you."

"Why don't you just put them in my folder like all the other critiques?"

"In case you want to pull the story. There are a few changes you might want to make before sharing it more broadly with the other writers."

Pull the story? My heartbeat sped up. "What kind of changes?"

"Don't get me wrong—it's a great first draft," he said. "There are lots of things to love." He began reciting story points from the beginning, middle, and end of the story, highlighting things he liked about the plot, praising my choice of using first person viewpoint instead of third because I really put readers into the head of the character. It sounded like he really had read the whole story. My chest started to swell.

"But what's *wrong* with it?" I interrupted.

"Well, I'd rather go over those comments face-to-face, if we could."

I scowled. This felt like a trap to talk about what the story was *really* about—teen suicide, specifically mine. He was trying to rescue me. "You're just trying to coax me back to school."

"What teacher wouldn't?" He laughed. "Kim, listen to me. You're such a gifted writer. You have a talent worth nurturing, and I believe you can really go somewhere with this story."

A gifted writer—no one had ever told me that.

"You're just saying that because, you know, of the ending," I said.

"It's the truth. You're the best writing student I've ever had."

"You're young," I said. "You haven't had that many students yet."

"Take the compliment, kid."

I looked at the bottle of pills in my hands. "You really think I'm a gifted writer?"

"Absolutely. I can't wait to see you go to college where you can do some really serious work."

I turned the bottle in my hands. "I can't go to college, Mr. Brown. My parents don't have the money to send me."

"Most colleges have financial aid departments to help students. I'd recommend that you speak directly to the departments of the universities that you're looking at and see what opportunities are available at those specific schools. Plus, there are federal and state grants you can apply for, as well as school loans to help you with whatever you can't cover any other way."

"Can you still win scholarships and stuff, even if you're not at the top of your class?"

"Most students who receive financial aid don't have straight A's," he said.

"Really?"

"Really. With grades like yours, you'll be able to go to college, Kim. Trust me."

"A *good* university?"

"I'm sure you'll find a way. I know it seems overwhelming, but there's lots of help available to you."

I didn't say anything for a moment. I looked at the prescription bottle in my hands again.

"I scored B's in Physics and Calculus," I whispered. Tears welled in my eyes and then flowed down my cheeks. A huge knot formed in my throat and burned.

"I know. I passed out report cards."

"I—" My voice broke. "I was supposed to be valedictorian!" I sobbed.

"I'm really sorry this happened," he said. "Losing sucks."

"Yeah!"

He was silent for a moment. I sniffled.

"Have you ever watched those personal interest stories during the Olympics?" he asked.

"Huh?" I swiped at my nose. Tears ran and ran.

"The Olympics, you know, those personal interest stories when they profile one of the athletes who had a particularly tough journey to get to the games. Against all odds, they made it, and they're going for the gold. It's a once-in-a-lifetime dream for them, their one shot, boiled down to an event that might last thirty seconds."

"Yeah." Where was he going with this?

"Lots of them don't win the gold—or even the silver or bronze. We forget all about them. They go home, back to their lives. Maybe they try to compete again. Maybe they do something different. But they don't kill themselves. Even something that feels like a catastrophic failure isn't the end of the world. It's just a moment."

"But they still failed. How do they *live* with that?" My voice cracked. Why couldn't I stop crying?

"You only see failure. You only see that they went to the Olympics—and failed. But Kim. *They went to the Olympics!* How many people can claim that? Even if you go to the Olympics and end up being dead last, you're still at the top percentage in your sport because *you're at the Olympics.*"

"Uh-huh." I sniffled.

"You're not valedictorian, okay. So you're number two?"

"Four."

"So let's say that you're in the Top Ten of your class. You see that as failure? Really?"

"It's not valedictorian."

"Nope, it's not," he agreed. "But is that the only possible acceptable thing to you? Is life *absolutely not worth living* unless you are number one? You are unable to reframe your

240

idea of success to include Top Five or Top Ten. Everyone else in the class except Heidi Jones should just fall on their swords because their lives are meaningless since they're not valedictorian."

"No."

"Are you saying that this standard applies only to you? And if so, why?"

I sighed. Okay, I understood what he was trying to say. I didn't *like* it—but I understood. "How did this become a one-on-one class discussion topic, and am I going to be required to write an essay?"

"That sounds like an appropriate punishment for ditching school today."

Someone pounded on the front door. I stood up. "Someone's knocking on the door, hold on a second."

"I thought you were at the mall," Mr. Brown said.

I shoved the pills under my pillows before walking down the hall to the living room and peeking out the window. Elliot's car was parked behind mine in the driveway, and he stood on the front porch, looking mad. I sighed.

"I have to go," I said. "Someone's here."

"Are you going to be okay?"

"I'm fine." I kept looking at Elliot.

"Will you think about what I've said?" Mr. Brown asked.

"Yes."

"I want to see you before class tomorrow morning. Can you come early?"

"Okay. Bye."

I hung up. I put my phone in my pocket and opened the door.

"What are you doing here?" I asked.

"You promised you'd call me first." He pushed inside.

"I'm still alive, in case you haven't noticed." Yes, he was definitely angry.

"Only because Mr. Brown called and kept you on the phone," he said. "I knew something was up when you said 'Goodbye Elliot,' so I followed you and watched you leave school. Then I went by writer's corner on a hunch."

I dropped my eyes. I should have listened to my gut. Bad idea to leave the story.

"Since we'd been working together, I only had to read the last chapter to find out what was going to happen. I did that, and then I went to find Mr. Brown and convinced him to stall you. He just wanted to call the police, but I convinced him that this way was better. Be warned that he's on the phone with your mom right now."

I groaned.

"We don't have much time."

"Time for what?"

He grabbed my face with both hands and pulled it close to his. His eyes burned into mine. My stomach flip-flopped. His lips pressed against mine, softly. I closed my eyes and relaxed into his arms. His hands slid along the sides of my face, into my hair, pulling me closer to him.

My legs felt like they had no bones. I sagged into him. He chuckled and broke the kiss. "No time for this, as much as I'd like to," he said.

"Huh?" I looked at him.

"Show me your report card."

I hung my head. "I don't want to."

"Show me, or I'm dumping your bag on the floor."

I went to my backpack and unzipped one of the pockets. I pulled out the printout of my grades and handed it to him. He looked at it for a moment.

"You really believe that this is all you are? That this defines who you are?" he asked. He shook the piece of paper.

I shrugged. It certainly defined who I was *not*. I was *not* valedictorian.

"Trust me, *this* has nothing to do with who you really are. It says nothing about your kindness, your dark stories, or your sense of humor."

"That," I said, pointing to the paper, "has everything to do with my future. It represents everything I've worked for over the past four years. All the hours of studying. All the hours of homework and writing papers instead of goofing off with friends. All of it for nothing!"

"Getting a B is not the end of the world."

"I scored two of them, and yes, it is. How would you know? You aren't trying to be the valedictorian."

"You're right. I'm not. But, I score B's all the time, and nothing bad happens. Do you think that I have no future? Do you think that I'm destined to live in a box under a bridge?"

"It's not the same for you."

"Why not?"

"Your parents can send you to college if you want to go. Mine can't."

"You needed straight A's to win scholarships," he said.

"Right."

"And now that won't happen."

I nodded.

"How do you know?" he asked.

"Because I'm not valedictorian."

"But how do you know that you can't still win scholarships? Have you applied for any in your new status as a non-valedictorian? No! Report cards were just handed out today. You have *no idea* what's possible."

I stared at him.

He held up a finger. "I say…hold off on this suicide thing until you know *for sure* that you haven't been accepted into any colleges. If that's the real goal, then you're not out of the running yet. You've just suffered a setback. You're still okay. Write some essays and submit some applications. See what happens first."

"And if things still don't pan out…"

"We'll talk again." He pulled me into his arms. "What did Mr. Brown say to keep you on the phone?"

"He told me I was a gifted writer."

"You are."

I smiled into Elliot's shirt.

"I bet you'll be accepted into a bunch of colleges with writing programs," he said.

"My dad doesn't want me to study writing—except as a hobby. He told me to pursue a degree in something that I can make a living at, like medicine."

"It's not his choice."

"No, but it's his advice."

"You have to follow your dreams," Elliot said.

"I have to be able to earn a paycheck, too."

"My brother's miserable in college right now because he's doing what our parents told him to do instead of what he wants."

I shrugged. "I don't have to decide on a career right away. Most of the universities I've looked at have good writing programs, but also other programs. I might be able to do both."

A car pulled into the driveway, and gravel flew as it skidded to a stop. The door slammed.

"Uh-oh. Here comes your mom." He dropped his arms from me.

Her shoes stomped on the steps leading up to the porch. I backed away from him. She was going to be furious for being called home from work and losing money on this shift.

She threw open the door. "Kim! What's going on?"

I opened my mouth, but nothing came out.

"Report cards came out today," Elliot said.

She looked at my face. Disappointment flashed in her eyes. "Oh, honey." She knew. She already knew that I'd failed. My face crumpled, and tears began to fall.

She crossed the room in three steps and wrapped her arms around me. Her winter coat was damp with snow. I sobbed into her shoulder. "I scored two B's."

"It's okay," she said.

"I'm not valedictorian anymore."

"It's okay, it's okay. All I ever wanted was for you to do your best."

"My best wasn't good enough!"

"Your best is always good enough," she said.

I lowered my eyes and whispered, "I don't know how to tell Dad." I thought of him bragging about me to all his friends and calling me "The Brain." I'd ruined everything.

"Oh, honey." She squeezed me. "We can tell him together. It's going to be all right."

"I don't know what's going to happen now."

"I'll let you in on a secret." She grabbed my shoulders and held me at arm's length. "We never know what's going to happen."

I looked over to where Elliot had been standing. He was gone.

"I'm sorry you had to leave work, Mom. I'm okay. Mr. Brown called, and then Elliot came and…I'm okay."

She stared at me for a long moment. Then she sighed and took off her coat and boots.

"Mr. Brown called and told me what was going on," she said. "He also said that you've written a story that I need to read."

I raised my eyebrows. "You might not like it."

"Give me a try."

"Really, you want to read it?"

"Absolutely!"

I nodded. "Okay."

"Also…*you* might not like it, but…" She looked at me. "I'm going to call Russ and have him talk to you this afternoon. I'll give you my appointment."

"I don't really—"

"Non-negotiable." She stared at me. "Also, let's go to your room right now and have a little look around. It would help if you'd fess up and tell me what I'm looking for."

I suddenly couldn't believe any of this was happening. I felt so ashamed of what I'd almost done and what I now needed to show her. The shame was enough to make me wish I'd succeeded with it because I sure as heck didn't like walking down the hall to my room with her close behind, watching.

She turned on the overhead light. We looked at my room. Bed made, everything neat and tidy. I reached under the pillow where I'd shoved the pills when the phone rang. I handed both bottles to her.

"Where did you get this?" she asked.

I hung my head. "I called in a refill. I didn't think there was enough in the bottle in the bathroom cabinet."

"How long have you been planning this?" Her voice was very quiet.

"Since the first of October, when I began really messing up in Calculus."

"Oh, Kim." She began crying. "Why didn't you say something to me?"

"There wasn't anything you could do. It was all on me."

"No." She shook her head. "You're never alone. You always have help if you need it."

"I didn't know what else to do."

She hugged me again. "I don't know what I would have done if I'd lost you."

"I'm sorry, Mom."

"I'm sorry, too. I've been so caught up in my own stuff that I stopped seeing you. I didn't see that you were in trouble and needed help."

I nodded. My throat burned so much it was hard to swallow. "I love you, Mom," I whispered. They were words we never said to one another, but then again, we never hugged either.

She squeezed tighter. "I love you too, honey."

She held me for a long time, and we both cried. At last, she stepped away and went to make a phone call to her doctor.

23. Afterward

June 10

Mr. Brown gave an end-of-year party for the Writer's Club. Everyone met at his house for burgers and cake, and his wife talked us into giving her a private reading. I think he put her up to it since she worked at the hospital and probably had no interest in creative writing. Plus, Mr. Brown conveniently had a few extra copies of previous issues of *WordCrafters* lying around his house that we could use.

"Who wants to go first?" he asked.

"I will," Elliot volunteered.

He read my favorite poem of his, "Paris Goes to Harvard." He raised his voice to mimic the snotty rich girl's and made all of us laugh, and when he finished, everyone clapped.

"You're destined for Broadway, Elliot," Amy said.

"Maybe you should try writing a play over the summer," Mr. Brown said.

"You're giving me a summer *assignment*?" Elliot asked. "I thought this was a party."

One by one, the writers shared their poems and short stories out loud. We all knew the work already, but hearing them performed was a new and fun experience because everyone put personal expression into the reading.

Afterward, several people broke off and started a game of Pictionary. Others stood around talking. I went to the cooler for a can of soda and found Mr. Brown alone.

"Thanks for having us," I said. "This is really nice."

"I'm glad you're enjoying yourself."

I snapped the pop-top open.

"Did you have a chance to look through my comments on the latest revision of your story?" he asked.

"Yeah, thanks."

"I'm really proud of you. You've taken your writing to a new level."

"I'm surprised you like it—with the darkness and all."

"You've taken the darkness and made it bigger than yours," he said. "That's what makes great art. I hope you keep working on it."

"I'm going to. And I'm going to find a writing group at college so I can keep working with other writers, like this."

"Good, that's very good. Are you going to study writing then?"

"I still haven't decided yet. I don't have to declare a major in my first year, so I think I want to keep my options open and explore a little first."

He widened his eyes. "You? Going into something without a firm plan?" His mouth formed an O.

I took a drink and nodded, trying not to smile.

"How are you feeling these days?" he asked.

"Okay."

He tugged at his beard. "I wish I believed you."

"You can. I'm fine," I said. Even my ulcer was healing.

"The girl in your story keeps saying she's fine, too, but then she kills herself."

"Yes, but… The girl in my story never finds anything to hold onto. She loses hope."

"What do you hold onto?"

I looked across the room at Elliot. Mr. Brown followed my gaze. I liked Elliot a lot…maybe even loved him, but he wasn't what saved me. Not really. He wasn't what I held onto now. I could lose Elliot. Who knew what would happen between us once I moved away to college? For now, we were happy, and that was enough.

"My dreams," I said. "I was accepted to my first-choice college—with financial aid. I thought that couldn't happen unless I was valedictorian, but that wasn't true. I didn't have to be perfect. There was still a way forward for me."

"Why doesn't your character see that there's a way for her, too?"

"I don't know."

"Well, you'd better find out. You're the author. You have to know everything."

I stared at the ground for a long minute. "It's because of the depression. She's too depressed to see a way out. It's too dark for her."

"Then you need to make that clear in the story."

I nodded. "You're right."

"How were you able to see through the depression?"

"For a long time, I couldn't."

"Have you talked to anybody about it? A doctor, maybe?"

"Yeah."

He looked at me.

I cleared my throat. "My mom takes me to someone."

"Good. That's nothing to be ashamed of, you know."

"Yeah, I know." But that didn't mean I felt like talking about it with anyone. "I should go."

"Okay, just one more thing. I want to give you my address. If you ever have trouble like that again and can't see your way out, or if you just want some help with a story, write to me. I'll be here for you."

"Okay, thanks."

"You're a very bright student and a talented writer. I'm sure you're going to go very far in life, Kim."

Our class assembled for high school graduation in the park across the street from the courthouse. Folding chairs formed white lines on the grass. Trees provided shade for the occasion. Donna and I sat together in our black caps and gowns, but as a top honors graduate, I also had a special red sash around my neck.

Donna leaned over and whispered, "What I wouldn't give for a cigarette right now."

"You'd set your little tassel on fire."

"These bobby pins are digging into my scalp, and this stupid little hat is giving me a really bad hair day."

"You look fine," I said, giggling. "Shh."

"No way am I taking it off and throwing it into the air after spending all morning trying to clamp the damn thing on my head."

I covered my mouth and tittered some more. On the stage, our principal droned into the microphone. At last the horrible event arrived: someone else was going to deliver the valedictorian speech.

Heidi walked up to the podium and smiled at the crowd. As she quoted portions of Robert Frost's poem, "The Road Not Taken," and talked about the choices we would make at the forks in our own life roads, Donna leaned over and whispered, "Blah, blah, blah. Where does she get off trying to give us all this sage advice? She's never been five miles past the state line."

I giggled. It should have been me up there, giving that speech. I had worked so hard for all these years. Losing sucked.

On the other hand, I was glad that I could relax and not have to stand in front of all these people. I didn't like public speaking anyway.

I watched Heidi glance at her notes and then lean toward the microphone. She looked so perfect up there with her curly hair and her straight-A GPA, but I knew that it was an illusion. Things hadn't worked out exactly as she'd planned either. Her boyfriend broke up with her at the end of football season. She hadn't been admitted into her first-choice school. Both of us took some hits during this competition.

At least high school was over. I'd done my best, and I'd been accepted into a good university—with enough scholarship money to be able to pay tuition, room, and board for my first year. After that, who knew? I'd work hard and do my best.

When the valedictorian speech concluded, another student sang a solo. She took center stage and belted an amazing version of "On My Own" from *Les Miserables* that stunned everyone. Here was this shy girl who'd been the silent (practically invisible) pianist for the concert choir since seventh grade, suddenly coming forward in the final hour and showing everyone that she had this gift inside of her all along and that she was so much more than we'd ever imagined.

I couldn't wait to find out what beautiful thing might be hiding inside me.

Khristina Chess lives with her husband and various pets in Huntsville, Alabama. By day, she works for an international software company, but in the wee hours of the morning, she writes novels.

Visit her online at www.khristinachess.com.

Made in the USA
Monee, IL
06 February 2022

90791711R00152